Praise for:

Signed, Mata Hari

"In *Signed, Mata Hari*, Yannick Murphy once again treats us to her luscious signature lyric style, its whispers and perfumes, in this time- and space-bending tale of the famous dancer and accused spy."
—Janet Fitch

"[An] alluring novel . . . hypnotic [and as] softly poetic as it is insistent."
—*Publishers Weekly* (Starred Review)

"Unself-consciously sensual and achingly beautiful, [*Signed, Mata Hari* consists of] short, exquisite, though never precious, chapters refined almost to a sequence of prose poems. [This] is a profound and profoundly beautiful novel, one that forcefully renews literary fiction's claim to be a laboratory of the human spirit."
—*Los Angeles Times*

" [A] seductive narrative . . . Murphy has fashioned a mesmerizing novel that creatively reimagines the life of one of the most notorious, and perhaps overvilified, women of all time."
—*Booklist*

"[A] wondrous novel, *Signed, Mata Hari* [is] exquisite and lush fiction."
—*The Boston Globe*

"Murphy writes like a dream, with vivid sensory descriptions.
—*The Dallas Morning News*

Here They Come

"This is a hell of a book. You might not be able to finish *Here They Come* in one sitting, but it will haunt you till you do. What detail! What characters! I can imagine both Jane Austen and Raymond Carver poring over this masterly novel."
—Frank McCourt

"Yannick Murphy's long-awaited *Here They Come* is a unique combination of rare linguistic lyricism with brutal and brilliant prose. It is an unrelenting portrait of family, terrifying for its honesty, its willingness to be ugly and elegant. Haunting."
—A.M. Homes

"In thick, poetic prose that edges toward stream of consciousness and is peppered with slightly surreal details, Murphy creates a world as magical and harrowing as the struggle to come to grips with maturity."
—*Publishers Weekly* (Starred Review)

"Murphy flawlessly captures a child's-eye view of a battered society and a battered family. The spare elegance of her prose contrasts so jarringly with the sordid physical landscape that it inspires an unsettling sense of disconnect, which is almost certainly the point. Most impressive of all is Murphy's remarkable use of language, the expressive way she puts together ordinary words and images to create surprisingly lovely and moving metaphors . . ."
—*Los Angeles Times*

"With remarkable restraint and lyrical prose, Murphy builds a novel moment by moment, showing us a strange world through the eyes of a girl who thinks nothing of it. How refreshing it is . . . to see a fictional adolescent who can be precocious without ever being dear."
—*Time Out Chicago*

"Especially satisfying is [Murphy's] ability to distill complex observations into concise paragraphs. . . Like a satisfying meal, you lean back and let [the novel] settle down, and you feel like you've taken in something good."
—*See Magazine*

The Sea of Trees
A *New York Times* Notable Book

"Murphy . . . offers a vision that is deeply subjective without being deeply interior. Her story unfolds through a dreamlike progression of glinting surfaces, telling gestures and precisely rendered moments in which matter-of-fact horror butts up against absurdist hilarity. . . Murphy imbues her world, ultimately, with a lush timelessness, shot through with surprising buoyancy and hope."
—*The New York Times*

"Yannick Murphy's first novel describes, with an eye for both beauty and irony, [the story of] and young girl's . . . realization that home is no longer a physical place: . . . a poetic narrative of strength and survival."
—*Bomb*

Stories in Another Language

"Murphy's fictional debut evinces a deadpan voice that powerfully taps the interior world of emotions and thoughts. . . [She] masterfully recreates childhood games and family idiosyncrasies, and her keen eye for small, mundane details captures the likes of bumper stickers and stretch marks."
—*Publishers Weekly*

IN A BEAR'S EYE

IN A BEAR'S EYE

Stories by
Yannick Murphy

DZANC
BOOKS

DZANC BOOKS

1334 Woodbourne Street
Westland, MI 48186

www.dzancbooks.org

Some of these stories orignially appeared in the following places:
"Find Natasha" in *The Quarterly #26*; "Jesus of the Snow" in *The Quarterly #27*, "In a Bear's Eye" in *McSweeney's #18*; "Walls" in *AGNI online magazine;* "The Lost Breed" in *McSweeney's #21;* "Into the Arms of the Man on the Moon" in *Conjunctions #12*; "The Story of the Spirit" (First published as "The Light") in *The Quarterly #4*; "The Fish Keeper" in *The New Gothic, a Collection of Contemporary Gothic Fiction (*Random House*);* "Pan, Pan, Pan" in *Conjunctions #49*; "Lester" in *The Quarterly #24*; "The Only Light to See By" in *The Quarterly #5*; "The Beauty in Bulls" in *The Quarterly #9*; "Kato and the Indians from Here" in *The American Voice #37*; "Aunt Germaine" in *Vestal Review #30*; "Is This a Land, a Continent, Can It Be Conquered?" in *Story Quarterly #27*; "Abalone, Ebony and Tusk" in *The Santa Monica Review*; "Legacies" in *Listen Up 2007*; "Whitely on the Tips" in *Epoch 56:2*; "Our Underwater Mother" in *Conjunctions #20*; "Delaware" in *The Malahat Review #75*; "Ready in the Night" in *The Quarterly #19*.

Published 2008 by Dzanc Books
Book design by Steven Seighman
Author photo by Clark Hsiao

06 07 08 09 10 11 5 4 3 2 1
First Edition February 2008

ISBN – 13: 978-0-9793123-1-1
ISBN – 10: 0-9793123-1-0

Printed in the United States of America

For Hank, Louisa, and Kit

Table of Contents

𝒞𝓈

FIND NATASHA

*I*t's covered in glass where we live.

"Skylights galore" our father said to our mother before we moved in.

But when we moved in, our mother walked up and down the place. "I'm nervous," she said to our father. "Places to live are supposed to be made out of tar and shingles, not glass. I can't sleep in a greenhouse. I'm not a tomato. I like possibility - waking up in the morning and thinking maybe it's raining and maybe it's not. Who needs to look up through a window when all there is to see is sky?" our mother said. "You know, Rog," she said, "nature can be avoided." Then she picked up a pot from off a box still unpacked and she threw the box at him. It ended up not hitting him but breaking a fish tank filled with my sister's mice.

The mice stayed there in the broken tank with glass all around them.

My sister shrieked.

"Rasputin! Boris! Natasha!" she yelled. "Hey, are you mice all right?"

"Whatever's good you got from me," our mother said to us when our father left the place and took off down the street on his bicycle.

"Like what?" my sister said.

"Square shoulders," our mother said. "Each of his slope down like a bent-necked pack mule stopped at a spring on a long stretch from home."

"Don't go out there," our mother told us.

So we stayed in the hall, sliding our backs around curves and hitting metal clips on mail boxes. Sometimes night was one long word game we played. It was Ghost or Pig or it was Botticelli.

One of my sister's mice escaped from the fish tank when my sister was once changing the shavings. "Natasha, Natasha, Natasha," she whispered all that night, walking back and forth in the house, holding out cheese in her hand.

In the morning it was raining, and we heard the drops hitting hard on our skylights.

"On other roofs it's falling like rose petals - but here it is raining like stones," our mother said.

But our father said to our mother, "You liked the last place? Those men on the street and the fires in barrels?"

Our mother said, "When I looked down at least I could see what was going on in the city."

What we've got under us here is a neighbor who has set up his place like a movie house with rows of old chairs whose legs are unbalanced. The neighbor has people come in and pay at his door and sit in his broken chairs to see the movies. All night we lay in our beds trying to listen to the movie voices. It is like people trapped in our floors.

Our mother takes a pot and bangs on the boards.

"Bogie! Bacall! Fuck 'em all!" she yells and she cries.

In the morning when we use the dented pot, it rocks back and forth on the burner of the stove.

In our place nothing is set up in rows. Even where we watch TV, the chairs are in a circle and the TV is in the circle with us as if we were going to ask the TV what it thought about books, about politics, wars, TV shows, electricity.

Sometimes we think we hear Natasha at night. Late, after the neighbor has finished showing his movies, we think we can hear Natasha chewing our beds.

"No difference to your Natasha, food or this house," our mother says.

Our mother goes to the kitchen, bringing her drink with her and saying how good she feels, how the fat bastards of the world could come knocking now at her door and she'd be nice to them, the crud. "I'd sheath my blade, sign peace papers, tape back together ripped pix of your father and me. I'd — God, " she says, "there's nothing to eat!" and she is at the icebox throwing old lettuce, a butter wrapper, an open can of tomato paste out behind her and onto the floor. Then she sits down on all the crap in front of the icebox and drinks her drink.

"Call your father!" she screams. "Break his heart! Tell the bastard it's not only nighttime outside, but it's nighttime inside, that the glass house he sent us to live in is coming fucking apart. No, better yet, find Natasha," our mother screams, "she's your man."

JESUS OF THE SNOW

*I*n Spain I knew a boy from Jaen. There his family picked the olives from the olive trees. The boy would not leave the house in the high hot sun and instead he would stay inside and look out at the hills and he would see his mother and father reaching up and coming back down to pick the olives from the trees. The way one would reach up while the other went down, the boy thought that his mother and father moved like a wave and that the hill they were on was the ocean.

This boy from Jaen says he would like to live in the caves in the mountains made by the gypsies, and with him he would bring some books and one loyal dog. He says he would spend his nights looking at the luna.

"Luna llena," he says.

The boy from Jaen has fallen in love with me. He is dark like a Moor. His name is Jesus. And the taken name from his mother is Jesus of the Snow.

In his town the women make their own chorizo and Jesus of the Snow has brought me the chorizo his mother has made. "It comes in strange shapes because casings of pigs are not always the same size," Jesus of the Snow says. "Oh, there was the pig," Jesus of the Snow says, "who stayed in the bar and took walks down the street and back into the bar," Jesus of the Snow says. "He was a fat pig," Jesus of the Snow says, "and the men gave him beer and olives and put a hat on his head."

The way the Andalusians do it is they drop their esses. So to say more or less, they say ma o meno. And now I still cannot say more or less without wanting to say instead ma o meno. "So ma o meno," Jesus of the Snow says, "the pig was our mayor. People went to him. A man went to the pig and told the pig that his wife wanted to leave him and go to the city. So what, asked the man of the pig, should I do? The pig said nothing and the pig stayed where he was under the table in the bar by the man's dusty feet, dusty from work in the olive fields where it seldom rained, and the man talked to the pig and then he got up and went home and he did nothing to his wife when he got there - the same as the pig had done nothing. The wife never left the town of Jaen for the city, and the men in the bar dropped olives to the floor for the pig to eat and straightened the hat on the pig's head. Ma o Meno," Jesus of the Snow said, "that is how the story goes."

Jesus of the Snow drives me to Mongo.

Up on Mongo we are close to the stars.

"This is a night of special constellations," Jesus of the Snow says. "A night so star-filled, must it not have a name?"

Jesus of the Snow sits me on the wet hood of the car.

I lean back.

The windshield is my pillow.

Jesus of the Snow gets up next to me.

"It is nights like these," Jesus of the Snow says, "that people go to kill themselves."

"What?" I say.

But he does not hear me, I think, because to hear someone on Mongo you have to shout or you have to whisper because the ocean is so loud up against the cliff.

Jesus of the Snow puts his mouth to my mouth. He whispers into my mouth, "I want to scream."

"Home of Dali," Jesus of the Snow says and spreads out his arms across the bar.

In Cadaques, the bars stay open late. We order champagne and ham and tomato on bread.

"You can see Dali everywhere here," Jesus of the Snow says. Jesus of the Snow's teeth are as white and square as the tiles on this floor of Dali's town. "Enough of this," Jesus of the Snow says, and we go. We walk where boats are tied. On a pier, we take off our clothes and dive from the cement into the water. We paddle our way between boats whose lines creak. Jesus of the Snow comes up between my legs. He spreads them apart with his hands pointed as if at his prayers. I hold his head there. Is this what he wants? Perhaps he wants to lose himself where olives cannot grow.

You can see the spire of the church in Cadaques from any-where in town. It is an eye that watches us while we eat the berried lobsters that the fishermen have trapped at the sun-up of today.

"In Jaen," Jesus of the Snow says, "it is the pig that people imagine is spying on them while they work the olive fields or when they wake up because of a noise in the room. Wherever you go," Jesus of the Snow says, "you have a Mona Lisa on the wall."

Radios put out on the street by the proprietors of stores play the songs of the kings along the ramblas.

My lover has my hand. We tarry at the windows. My lover is looking in. He looks at leather shoes and cabled sweaters. "The things I want for you are not here," he says. "I must give you God," he says, "now that you are strong enough to have Him."

I give Jesus of the Snow a gun.

We shoot at chameleons creeping across the sides of buildings.

"Look," Jesus of the Snow says, "the walls are Grecian blue, so that when the animals die, they die the Grecian blue."

But I only see the horror where the sunflowers are facing me and being pecked for the seeds in their hearts by birds come down from the chimney tops and roosting posts nearby.

"Stop looking," my lover says, and tells me his plans for us to take a mountain dog with us to the gypsies in a cave.

"I would lie on the dog in the mouth of the cave," Jesus of the Snow says. "I would hear the dog heart beat under me. I would watch the lights of the town down below shudder in my stallion's eyes."

"What about the pig?" I say. "Can't we take the pig with us to the cave? The pig could counsel us," I say.

Jesus of the Snow takes hair that has fallen into my face and puts it behind my ear.

"Come with me," he says.

"Distance," my lover says, "is what you get when you live in a place and then you leave it."

We are always leaving Cadaques. The road is so curved that when we turn to look back behind us all that we see is the road we have traveled and not the town of Cadaques or even the spire of its church.

The fog comes.

We stop the car at a guard rail and we get out and stand and look for a view down below.

It is time to kiss.

Jesus of the Snow puts his hands to my tetas, holding these parts of me up as if they are in danger of falling down or of coming off me and getting lost in the fog.

"Men of the cloth," Jesus of the Snow says, looking at street sellers who are selling table linen embroidered and laced with the thread of Morocco. We buy goods made out of things. My lover buys a gourd. I buy a hair ring which I wear at night when we go into the bars to listen to men sing while they cry and pour anise into their mouths. Jesus of the Snow says he does not know what the words are that the men sing, but that, ma o meno they are the songs of the heart and its openings and closings.

His home now is stone. Past his maid bent soaping the hard staircase steps and the tiled landings in his French-windowed room. Abuela in the room next to his sits eating carrots and looking at the wall.

"You two," she says, "where do you think you are going?"

"Far!" yells Jesus of the Snow, taking my hand and pulling me down the hall. My lover shouts, "Andalusia."

"Take a sweater," Abuela says. "The days are hot, but the nights, ah."

In Jesus of the Snow's room he puts a gun to my head.

"What color will you turn after you are dead?" he says.

"The color of this room," I say.

"And if I kill you out there?" he says.

"The sky," I say.

"And under the water?" he says.

"Myself," I say.

"And in Peru?" he says, and cocks the gun.

I cannot picture Peru. I can only picture mountains with steps leading up. "Sometimes," I say, "I can see a man working in the garden. He is tying stalks to dowels, walking through the rows and looking up at the sun. He is a wrinkled man, and I think that it is in the garden where he will die."

"Yellow," Jesus of the Snow says. "Peru is yellow."

My lover lifts up my skirt, pushes open my legs, and gets the gun to go up inside me.

It is so cold.

"Will you miss me when you are yellow?" he says.

Let me tell you of the time I go back to visit Jesus of the Snow the summer when all of Spain seems to me to be in the ocean. People are floating on their backs in the water, swimming far away from shore.

"Look at me," I say to Jesus of the Snow. "It is all the dairy in the States. It has made me fat in the bazongas, can't you see?" I say.

"Ma o meno," he says.

I see boys are part way out hollering into the water, making animal sounds that carry far along the beach.

"I have got girls," he says. "Some of them are good girls. Some of them are from up around here. Some are dark and from down there. There are Madrilenas who I let talk on and on because I listen to the sounds of their tongues on their teeth. When you left," he says, "I went with them all."

A fat man calls out near to us, "Coco—coco rico," and I see that he holds a knife whose blade is curved.

"Extranjera," my lover says. "You no come from anywhere."

The man with the knife comes at me.

Jesus of the Snow stands up from the mat we are on and walks toward the water, toward where all the Spanish are.

"Wait!" I call.

The man with the knife is coming.

I am so cold. I am in Spain, on some coast named for valor, but I am so cold.

Jesus of the Snow dives into a wave and is gone.

The man with the knife sings to me — "Coco, coco rico," he sings. I cannot see the Spanish in the water because the man is singing. "Coh, coh, coh, coh, ricoooooooh." He puts the knife in my hand and puts a coconut down on a board on the sand. I put the knife down on the coconut and the milk spills off the board and the sand turns black. But if I have pieces of coconut do you think they will come to me? Their manes wet? Their gait strange in the sand?

IN A BEAR'S EYE

*S*he heard the bear. It hooted like an owl, only lower, sounding like an owl far down in a well or in a cave. She looked out the window. There it was, in the field above the pond on its hind legs. It shook the apples from the apple tree. Her boy did not look up at the bear in the field. He was by the pond. The bear was not so close but neither was he far away. If the bear had wanted to, the bear could run to the boy and the bear could be on her boy in no time at all, in the time it took an apple to fall from the branch and onto the field.

She ran outside with her gun.

Her boy had brown hair that over summer had turned almost blond. In the light of the setting sun she imagined how her boy's hair would look golden, how when he moved about, as he never kept still, how the color of his hair would surely catch anyone's eye, even a bear's.

When she was a girl she wanted her hair to turn that color. She cut lemon wedges and folded them around the strands of hair and pulled down on the lemon wedges, all the way to the ends. She would then lie down and bathe in the sun. She spread her hair out behind her on the towel. The strands were sticky. There was lemon pulp clinging to them in places. Bees flew close to her hair. The color stayed a light brown.

The gun was heavier than she had remembered. There was probably some muscle in her arm that was once stronger when she had carried the gun with her husband through the woods. They had hunted grouse every season. Now the muscle was weak. To get to her boy she knew that she would have to first crouch behind the rock wall and then, like a soldier, she would have to run and hide behind trees. She would have to be in some way like a snake. Serpentine, her pattern. Isn't that what a soldier would say? Serpentine, she would have to run down the line of trees that bordered the field for a few hundred feet. She did not think she could do it. She would eventually be seen. The bear would stop shaking the apple tree and look around, sniffing the air. The bear might come at her.

Her husband was the one who always shot the grouse. He was a good shot. She always aimed too high. Her husband, while she was aiming, would put his hand on top of her gun, to lower it down, but still she never shot a grouse.

The boy took some small rocks from the pond's shoreline. He stood up and threw them into the water.

"Sit down," she said out loud in a whisper that didn't sound to her like her own voice.

The boy was not doing well in school. He liked to read during class. Beneath the desk he would hold an open book. A book about beavers or silk moths or spiders. The teacher sent him home with notes for his mother. The notes said the boy must pay attention. Her boy would sometimes read to her from his books while they ate dinner. There were things she had never learned as a girl. A silkworm female moth is born without a mouth. It does not live long enough to eat. It only lives long enough to mate and lay its eggs before it dies. Her boy would stop and show her the pictures. She would shake her head. She was amazed at how much she had never learned as a girl her boy's age. Was she just too busy squeezing lemon wedges onto her hair? Her boy never said he was sad that his father, her husband, had died. But she knew he was sad. Her husband was like a book that could talk. At the dinner table he would tell their boy about science and math. He talked about zero. "Zero scared the ancients," her husband said. "No one wanted to believe that there could be nothing."

He walked into the ocean one day and he did not stop walking. She liked to think he was still walking under the water. Skates stirred up sand and rose to the surface as he walked by them. Water entered his shirt cuffs and his shirt back ballooned. She and her boy sometimes talked about it. Her boy said how the hair on his head must be floating up and wavering like the long leaves of sea plants. Her boy said how his father must be reaching out to the puffer fish, wanting to see them change into prickly balls. His father must be touching everything as he walks, the craggy sides of mouths of caves where groupers lurk and roll their eyes, the white gilled undersides of manta rays casting shadow clouds above him. "My father must be in China by now," the boy said to his mother.

China because after he had died and the boy and the mother cleared out the father's drawers, they found a travel brochure for China. They had no idea the father was interested in going to China, but the words *"See the wall"* were written on the outside of the brochure.

The mother now saw how the sun was going behind the hillside. Its last rays hit the black steel of her gun and it hit the very top of her boy's hair before it sunk down. The bear was finished. It had knocked almost all the apples to the ground. He began to eat them. The mother thought how the boy would be safe now, the bear would eat and then leave and she would not have to run closer to the bear, going from tree to tree, looking for a shot she would probably miss because her husband was not there to put his hand on her gun, pushing down, keeping her from aiming too high.

Not long ago the boy's teacher had come to see her. She held open the screen door for the teacher and told her to come in. They sat in the kitchen and the teacher asked the boy if she could speak with his mother alone. The boy nodded and slid a book off the kitchen table and left the room. The mother could hear the boy walk up the stairs and close the door to his room.

"Your boy is a smart boy," the teacher said. "The death of his father must have come as a shock. But still," the teacher said, "there is school."

She looked into her refrigerator to offer the teacher something. There wasn't much. She hadn't been to the store in days. She opened the bottom bin and found two lemons. She took them out and put them on the table where they rolled for a moment. The mother got her wooden chopping board and placed the lemons on it and cut each lemon in four. She pushed the chopping board toward the teacher. "Please, have some."

The teacher did not say anything. After a while the teacher said, "I'm sorry. I'll come back another day to talk about your son." When the teacher left, the mother went upstairs to her boy. He was reading a book about spiders. Together they lay on his bed and looked at the pictures.

She would take her boy on a trip. They would go to China. They would see the wall. They would look for signs of him. She had yet to tell the teacher how her boy would miss days of school, even weeks.

Now, at the pond, the boy thought he would try it. He walked in slowly. The brown water filled his tennis shoes. It was cold. The boy knew from his books that beavers had flaps of skin behind their front teeth. They could shut the flaps when underwater, sealing the water out of their mouths and lungs. When the water came above the boy's eyes and finally over his head, the boy imagined he had these flaps. He opened his eyes underwater. The darkness was like four walls all around him. Maybe he could reach out and touch them.

The bear stopped eating. It sniffed the air and lifted its head. It went toward the pond. When it walked it looked like a man who was sauntering. She did not know before how bears hooted like owls, how they sauntered like men. She followed it. She did not run from tree to tree. She ran in a straight line. "No, no, you'll never shoot anything running at it like that," she could hear her husband say. Where was her boy? Where was her husband?

She saw ripples in the pond where her boy had gone in and then she noticed that the bear was looking at her. Its upper lip was curled. It had white on its chest, the shape of a diamond, but not perfect, a diamond being stretched, a diamond melting. She let the gun drop. She ran fast through the milkweed. The butterflies flew ahead of her. She ran past the bear. She dove into the water on top of the ripples made by her boy. She wanted to save him. She wanted to tell him he did not have to drown. She swam down, wishing she could call to him underwater, wishing she could see through the black silt. She had not taken a breath before she went down and she could not believe she did not need one. She thought for a moment how everyone must be wrong, there was no need to hold your breath underwater. She now knew it. She thought her boy knew it too. They had both found out a secret. She could stop thrashing about in the water now, looking for her boy. He would come up and out when he was ready. When she came to the surface she realized the pond was shallow. She was standing with the water only coming to her hip.

Her boy was on the other side of the pond. He was sitting on a large flat rock on the shore. He was holding something in his hand. The bear was watching them, his lip no longer curled. She walked to her boy while still in the water. It dragged her shirt sleeves and her pant legs behind her. She moved her hair away from her eyes.

The boy had mud in his hand that he had scooped from the bottom of the pond.

"What's that?" she said.

"Maybe some gold," the boy said, moving the mud around and poking at it in his palm.

"Look over there," the mother said, pointing to the bear. The bear turned and sauntered away.

"Yes," said her boy. "I saw him ages ago. He likes the apples from our apple tree."

That night she told the boy that maybe they had better not go on their trip to China after all. There was school to think about. The boy nodded. "All right," he said.

She thought how she missed her husband. She thought how she would now miss him the way other women must miss their dead husbands. She would wear his shirts. Isn't that what other women did? They took long walks and thought about their husbands and when they sweat the smell that came up to them was not the smell of themselves but the smell of their dead men?

WALLS

*T*he year Josefina tried to climb the walls in her sleep, my father learned how to swim. In the mornings Josefina would put her bruised fingertips into olive oil and then she would let the dogs lick them while she stood on the balcony and yelled down to my father in the pool. At first he kept his head above the water, but Josefina, after the dogs had licked her fingertips clean, went down to my father and pushed his head under and straightened his back and held his legs taut.

It was all for pelota. My father said opposing muscles were what would make him stronger and faster and see the ball better. Josefina said it would keep him from drowning.

My mother wrote to us from France saying we would have swim parties when she returned, she would buy us new suits and for Josefina, a strong rope and some gloves.

Josefina decided that what would keep her from climbing the walls in her sleep was if she never went to bed. So all day and all night Josefina would clean. She cleaned the jars of spices and she cleaned the broom and she cleaned the dogs and she cleaned the pelota balls and she cleaned the walls and she cleaned my father and she cleaned me and she cleaned herself and while washing her hair in the tub she fell asleep and in her sleep she climbed out of the tub and with soap still in her hair, she tried to climb her freshly cleaned walls. In the mornings the dogs licked the water off the floor and Josefina pulled them back by their tails.

My mother wrote to us again, saying she wouldn't be home for Christmas, but that she was sending us the suits. Small anchors were sewn into my father's suit.

"I won't wear this," my father said, "I might sink down to the drain."

Soon my father won every game of pelota that he played and he let the pool water drain and Josefina was found at night trying to climb up the sides of the pool, the dogs barking by the sun chairs above.

In the mornings, Josefina's fingernails were blue from the paint in the pool and the bread she served us was blue and her face was blue from where she had touched it with her hands.

After my mother's letters stopped coming my father began to lose his games of pelota. Josefina bought herself gardener's gloves.

"My fingertips are losing their swirls," she said and the walls in the swimming pool and the walls in our house had Josefina's marks all over them.

"Come here," Josefina said to me, and I went up to her and she took my hand and put it in the olive oil and she made me press my hand up against the walls saying she didn't want to be alone on her climbs.

My father said, "Come here" to me also and he took me to the beach and we watched the waves and then he took off his shirt and then his pants and his socks and his shoes and he went for a swim. When he came out I dried his back for him and then he let me ride on his shoulders and I smelled ocean salt in his hair while we walked along the streets. He took me to where he played pelota and he asked me to bend down and kiss the floor on the side where he played. After I stood up I had dirt on my lips.

"Let's drink coffee," he said and he took me to one of his bars and he sat me on the table and had me shake the hands of his friends.

At home we found blood on the walls, but we could not find Josefina. We looked in the pool, and there was blood on its walls, but Josefina was not there. We found the dogs, and there was blood on their coats.

"Where is Josefina?" my father asked the dogs, and the dogs whined and went in circles.

I found the gardener's gloves on the floor. My father took them and he left to find Josefina. I stayed behind with the dogs and after petting their bloodied coats I put my hands up against the walls and stood back to watch my handprints there.

I ate bread with olive oil poured over it and walked around our house. I went into my father's room and saw the swim suit with the anchors on it lying on his floor. I went to the side of the bed where my mother used to sleep and I kissed the sheet and my lips left an olive oil stain.

The dogs followed me and waited for me to give them the crust from my bread, which I did and I threw it out from off the balcony and I watched them hunting out the bread with their noses in the dead leaves at the bottom of the pool.

My father came back with one of his friends. Together they opened all the doors in our house, looking for Josefina in places where we kept the food, our clothes, and my father's gear for pelota.

We found Josefina in the hospital. There was tape and gauze up and down her arms. She told my father she would clean the house when she got back and my father took up her arm and said with an arm like a stick like that he might have some luck in a game.

"Your mother could do that," my father said and on the beach he pointed to a woman swimming like a dolphin, her back moving like the rolling waves and her kicks sending up foam. When the woman came out of the water I walked over to the towel where she lay and watched how her breasts and her belly moved up and down. Then I went to my father and sat between his legs and poured sand over his knees and he closed his knees together so that I couldn't move. I tickled his sides and his knees came apart and I fell onto him, holding the hair on his chest between my fingers and him telling me to let go, that it hurt.

At night I would strap Josefina into her bed. With rope my father ran through the frame I would section her in three and tie knots around her. Josefina's black hair, after having been braided all day, spread out onto her pillow in waves that fell towards the floor. Josefina would lift up her head and look down at my work.

"Tie the legs tighter," she would say, "those are the ones that think I'm a goat and can climb."

The next year my father did not learn how to do anything and Josefina did not climb the walls in her sleep. I went to school and learned how to spell. At home I stood on a chair and spelled all over the walls with my pens and wrote my mother long letters that I knew she couldn't help reading if she were ever to come back and walk into our home.

THE LOST BREED

We are in search of a breed that is most likely lost. The breed is a Mucuchies, said to have accompanied Simon Bolivar on his conquests. I have come to help the professor, his wife, and the girl whose brother will die. I will help ask people where a dog of this breed might be. I know a little of the language. I know "un poquito".

The Cadillacs should have been jeeps. We had reserved jeeps to travel the bumpy roads, to travel off the roads, through the frailejones plants that grew everywhere around where the farmers lived who kept dogs who might be the mysterious Mucuchies. At the airport, though, they did not have any jeeps for us to rent.

"No, No," I said in Spanish about the Cadillacs. "We must have jeeps. We need jeeps!" But of course, I only know "un poquito" and I did not know if there was a word for jeeps, so I said, "Heaps. We must have heaps!" thinking it sounded Spanish. But still, they did not make any heaps magically appear in their lot in the hot sun where the Cadillacs gleamed all in a row.

I have known the girl whose brother will die a long time. I have been to her house. I have sat on the wide porch with her. We have stood side by side cooking in the old farm kitchen where the warped boards lean in toward the stove and food set in the back of the pans cooks faster than in the front. I have known her boyfriend who whenever he is sitting pulls her down onto his lap so she is sitting on him and so I am used to seeing him with his face half covered by her sleeve as he peeks around her when he talks to others. I have not met her brother. But there is one story I know about him. How when they were younger he made a bomb and set it off in the bottom of their empty, leaf-filled swimming pool. The blue tile cracked. The leaves blew up and over the sides of the pool and throughout their New England town as if it were fall again, when really it was winter.

Oh, hell, her name is Alice, and yes, still, her brother will die.

The professor is Duncan, his wife is Charlotte. Duncan loves the price of gas in this country. After filling up the Cadillacs, he wants to fill them up again, just because it is so cheap. Charlotte takes pictures of us. We are standing in the road, asking farmers about their dogs. We are shown a box of puppies, the mother letting us come close. But the puppies look like Saint Bernards. "Mucuchies?" I ask.

"Sí, sí," the farmer says, the stubble on his chin flecked with flaking skin. The air up here is dry. We are close to the sun. Our cheeks turn red in one afternoon. The farmer shows us his terraced fields where potatoes grow that he will sell to burger chains back in our land.

Alice drives. She follows Duncan and Charlotte's Cadillac as Duncan drives and leads the way as we search for more dogs. I look at the map and read the guidebook. I tell Alice we should visit Pico Espejo, where it says in the guidebook we will find "eternal snow". "Or of course," I say, "we could visit Estado Barinas which is a major hunting place "with tiggers and dears" or there is also the forest of "permanent rain".

Alice says she is thirsty. She licks her lips. Duncan is not stopping. There are no signs of dogs in the town we are passing through. There is a church made entirely of stones. The church looks like children built it. The stones look like they teeter in the mountain wind. I tell Alice that the guidebook says that every year there is a re-enactment in the church. Every year Baby Jesus takes his first baby steps and Mary and Joseph rejoice, but every year Baby Jesus, because he now can walk, gets lost. "The painful Virgin asks for her lost baby in every door. 'My son is lost'," the guidebook says, "where might he be? I cry inconsolably. Take pity on me'. 'Go on,' the people answer her, 'your baby is not here.' Then the painful Virgin becomes angry. 'Give me back my baby,' she says to someone at their door. 'You are a thief,' she says."

"At last," Alice says when she sees Duncan turning off the road and stopping in front of a store. There are no lights inside the store. There are no fixtures on the ceiling, no lamps plugged into the walls. The store is only open when there is enough daylight for the customers to see the soda in small bottles, the flat salted fish beneath the glass counter top. The eyes of the fish are covered with the grains of crusted salt. Alice buys six of the small soda bottles, and drinks two while paying at the counter. We do not know the money. We lay our bills over the counter, the flat fish now hidden. We let the woman behind the counter take what she wants of our money. She slides out a bill. Her blouse is embroidered with orange, red, and yellow flowers. The flowers are so bright they seem to light up her store and make it easier to see what's for sale. Maybe she has been in the re-enactment at the church made entirely of stones. Maybe she plays the painful virgin.

Alice's house has connected rooms. You can walk from the kitchen to the living room to the dining room, through the study and back into the kitchen again. It saves time when you are looking for keys you cannot find, you never have to stop and turn around, you just keeping going in circles. Alice's boyfriend continues his conversation while walking through the rooms because he knows that even if Alice misses a word when he is in the room farthest from her, that she will hear the rest of what he has to say very shortly and she can easily guess what words she might have missed.

Duncan is at the gas pump smiling, shaking his head, not believing the price. Charlotte is taking pictures of the only dog she has found. It is small and brown and its legs so short and skinny they look like Slim Jims and when she reaches out it trots away. It is not a Mucuchies. It is not a dog Simon Bolivar would have taken into war. It could not have possibly trudged through eternal snow and perpetual ice on legs like Slim Jims.

We stay in a hotel for the night with a dining room that the guidebook says "overlooks the eternal snow and the perpetual ice." Duncan asks me to ask the waiter where all the dogs are in the town.

"All the dogs have gone," the waiter says.

"Gone where?"

"To the dump," the waiter says. "The dump outside of town. All the food they need is there."

"That's it," Duncan says. "We have to go to the dump at dawn. I bet that's when the town dumps their garbage. I bet that's where we'll spot a Mucuchies," he says.

At dawn we drive to the dump. In the distance the Andean mountains are purple, the tops bright white where the sun strikes the peaks before anything else on the land. In the half-light, standing on a hill of garbage that we realize is made completely of plastic coffee stirrers, we see the dogs come. Duncan has night-vision binoculars. "Are they Mucuchies?" we ask.

"Mucuchies, hell, no," he says. "They're mutts," he says. "But they have learned a great lesson, they are in perfect harmony with us. They eat our garbage," he says, and he continues to watch the dogs, all with the same Slim Jim legs gingerly walking over the hills of garbage, stopping to eat, their heads down, then up, like deer listening for hunters in the woods.

We do not find a Mucuchies. We travel south. Duncan wants to know what kinds of dogs live there. We stop on a bridge and see the bumpy head of a crocodile in river water. I read aloud from the guidebook, "The rerained water makes an ideal place where to enjoy acuatil sports." "One can see continuous lightning without thunderclaps." The crocodile slides beneath the water. We climb back into our Cadillacs.

There is a place to see birds in the rain forest. We find it on the map. We cannot go as far as the road goes into the rain forest. "If only we had Heaps" I say, "and not these low-riding Cadillacs." We park our Cadillacs on the side where the road begins. We begin to walk a little ways on foot.

Duncan has a bird book. We can hear the howler monkeys. We can see them sitting in the trees. "Look there," Duncan says. On the forest floor is a bright orange bird. Duncan looks through the bird book. "A Cock of the Rock," he says. He taps his finger on the page. "This bird is the rarest in the country." More of the orange birds join the first orange bird. They circle together. "A leck," Duncan says. "A leck of Cock of the Rocks." Charlotte takes a picture. The howler monkeys up above start to throw things at us. Leaves fall down onto our heads and shoulders. We walk back to our Cadillacs with bits of branches and seed pods in our hair. Charlotte protects the camera, keeping it under her shirt.

We get to our hotel in the evening. There are bugs that make ticking sounds as they fly in our room. There is a bug in the bathroom on the floor that Alice thinks I should step on. The body of the bug is as big and thick as a candied date. "You step on it," I say and Alice comes in to the bathroom and we stand looking at it and decide we can live with the bug.

In the morning Alice says she could use the beach. It is not too far. At the beach three boys come and sit on a boat with broken boards and they watch us. We are on our backs. We are taking in the sun. After a while, a woman comes and the boys make room for her and she sits with them and watches us. When we go for a swim, the woman tells the boys to stay on the boat with the broken boards and then she lifts up her skirt and walks in the water and watches us. Alice is good. She can ride waves all the way up to shore. All the way up to the woman's brown ankles.

That night we are in our beds. This is when it happens. This is when the phone rings and it is Alice's boyfriend. This is when Alice says "What?" into the phone and I think how maybe the boyfriend is walking through the connected rooms in Alice's house and she cannot hear the words he has said and she has to guess what the words are that were left in one of the rooms in her house. Then Alice sits up on her bed. Her face is very red. "He is dead?" she says. She has found the missing words. They have reached her now.

He was following his friend in a car on the road. The tire blew on the friend's car and so they stopped by the guard rail. He pulled his car behind his friend's car. He worked the jack. He turned the axle. He did not know a car with a drunk at the wheel would smash into his car and that he would be killed by the force of his own car pinning him against his friend's car. He did not know his sister would be in a hotel room and hear the news and stand at the window, pushing the curtain aside, to watch the continuous lightning strike over a hillside.

Charlotte could do it. Charlotte could sit with Alice on the end of the bed and hold her and rock her while she cried. Charlotte had children of her own and Charlotte had shoulders already knowing the feel of a face pressed into them and the strange sound a sob made there in the pit of her arm. I sat on the floor by the bathroom. I looked at the bug that looked like a candied date in the bathroom and then it began to crawl in my direction, as if to come and comfort me.

It was the end of our trip. We returned the Cadillacs we wished were jeeps back to the airport and there, in the rental parking lot, were two brand new jeeps that probably should have been ours and we wondered how our trip would have turned out different if we had had those jeeps instead of the Cadillacs and Duncan said it wouldn't have been different at all. Alice looked at the jeeps a while and I thought maybe she was thinking how it could have been different, but then she had been looking at things for a long time all day.

She had looked at a picture in the guidebook of the eternal snow a long time without even turning the page while I drove the

Cadillac to the airport. She had looked for a long time at an ashtray in a gift shop when we stopped for gas. She looked at it for so long, I was about to tell her to hurry. I wanted to tell her we shouldn't miss our plane, but then she finally took the hoof ashtray and brought it to the counter and paid for it, fanning out the money in her hands to the cashier so he would take what he needed. She bought it for her boyfriend, even though he didn't smoke. She held it in her lap on the ride to the airport. She smoothed down the hair on the leg of the steer so that strands of it covered the hard black hoof.

There were birders on the plane. The birders went through the aisles visiting one another. They pulled out white sheets of paper. They checked off birds they had seen on their trip. Alice nudged my shoulder and then, to one birder standing next to us in the aisle she said, "Excuse me." Then Alice smiled.

"Did you get a chance to see the Cock of the Rock?" she said.

"Well we flew out here specifically to see one, but we didn't. No one's seen the Cock of the Rock on a birding trip for a good ten years," the birder said.

"Really," Alice said. "We saw one," she said.

"No!" the birder said.

"Really, we saw more than one. We saw a leck," Alice said. The birder gasped.

"A leck!" he said. "My god, where?" he said. We had our map. We showed him where. "But we were there, we went for miles into the heart of that place!" he said.

By now all the birders who could surround our seats were surrounding us. They wanted to know exactly where we saw the bird. Alice told them we had Cadillacs, not Heaps. Alice told them we could not drive into the heart of the place because of the low riding Cadillacs. She said we hardly drove on the forest road. "We pulled off at the start of the road," she said. "We did not walk far at all," she said. "Maybe twenty yards or so into the trees," she said. The birders mouths were open. The birders wanted to turn the plane around. The birders quickly made a plan. The birders would land in our country, they would start another trip. They would rent Cadillacs this time, to hell with the Heaps they had rented. The Cadillacs made all the difference they reasoned. Alice smiled, "Yes," she said to the birders, "it very well could have been the Cadillacs."

When we landed, Alice's boyfriend was there to pick us up. While we waited for our bags to come off the carousel, Alice's boyfriend sat down, and he pulled Alice onto him so she was sitting on his lap. He peeked around her shoulder to talk to us. He asked Duncan and Charlotte about the Mucuchies breed and Duncan showed him photos of the dump and the dogs at the dump that lived there and who did not have an ounce of blood in common with any dog that may have traveled with Simon Bolivar while he conquered a country.

Years later, Alice's family and mine were invited to a Day of the Dead potluck dinner. Everyone brought the favorite meal of one of their relatives who had died. Other people at the party had spent hours cooking dishes like Chicken Marbella and veal medallions in white wine for their relatives.

"I'm lucky," Alice said to me in the kitchen. "I have it easy. My brother liked mac and cheese from a box."

Alice and I both had baby girls, and at one point during the dinner they were both hungry at the same time. Alice and I both excused ourselves and got up from the dining room table and went and sat in rockers in the living room at the same time. We both lifted up our shirts at the same time. When our milk let down at the same time, we knew it, and we started to laugh. We could not stop laughing and our baby girls still nursed, securely latched, the closest things to our shaking selves.

INTO THE ARMS OF THE
MAN ON THE MOON

*T*here is the man on the moon. Go to him. Get bread from him, drink his water. Take your dog Blue to him. Take your mother. She is skiing outside around the house. Stop her, tell her that Blue is going also. Take the gander, Henry. He is short in the legs. Leave me Iris. I have seen her eat feed in a pattern.

Tell the man on the moon I am out with the dogs. I have loaded them up. I am not without ointment for my lips. This is an occasion. Harnessed, the dogs are mindful of the bitch. Tell the man on the moon I think she will whelp seven. Ask him if he can know those kinds of things.

I will miss your hair. Cut some for me. Leave it inside my boot. When I pull it out, I will see summer. My foot will stay warm. Tell the man on the moon we have summer here. If he asks, show him your hair. If he asks about stars, laugh. If he asks again, show him your heart.

Your hair will not feel the same in my boot as it does on your head. Tell him how I would kill for you. You know the scream the rabbit makes when it is killed. It is the most frightening sound there is. This is only what I think.

The dogs are loaded up. Go look at them first. Tell me they remind you of the time we climbed the mountain. I am thinking of the mountain.

Ask him not to sleep with your mother, my wife. Try and draw next week. It always looks a little like last week. What is wrong with the pencils?

Take your mother's mittens. I could not bear to see them up on the hooks with the snow melting off them and her not here. Tell her to wear them when she meets the man on the moon. If he asks, say she is sick in the hands. Let me think about the mountain now.

I saw the bone in your foot. You took off your shoes and we rested and I saw a bone in your foot that I had never seen before. I thought you had put it there. It took you away from me. I was watching evolution. You were going down the line away from me. There is no bone in my foot like that bone in yours.

I will eat bark. I will pull your hair from my boot. I will see summer. Check the dogs. They tire when I talk about summer. Tell the man on the moon your father does not know what he is talking about. Tell the man on the moon your father would say he saw summer in his son's hair because it sounded good. Tell the man on the moon your father would kill for you. Tell him again. Tell him because your father sent you. Tell him to send back my goddamn wife. I like your foot. Open your ears. Tell the man on the moon we say things like that. Your foot is daring. It is breaking the line. My dogs are lying down. They are ready to go. I have to remember the ointment for my lips.

How many times have I done this?

There have been men who have done it with dolphins.

He is a stroke of luck. Yes, I am leaving you. Do not deny your foot. Show him what you are made of. Show him your teeth.

Tell people that I am crazy. Tell people that I have seen the man on the moon.

Go to him.

Ask him what will become of me.

Tell him your father doesn't know.

Lie to him.

Tell him you are dying and have to know. He will spread out his arms to you. He will offer you himself. I will look up. I will see happiness and safety and comfort above.

STORY OF THE SPIRIT

I am not old enough yet to say what I am going to say. And neither is she. But you become wise down in the kitchen when you are all smoking and the others are closing their robes in around themselves and telling stories. That is what she says. She also says her favorite story is the story of the spirit who clawed at the farmer's thatched roof all night long.

It is the story they often tell down in the kitchen, and every time she hears it she says she has grown a year older, and so afterward she celebrates and they make chairs for her out of their arms and walk her down the hall, their bare feet making sounds on the stone floor of the hall in the manner of children gone to get up and walk in the middle of the night.

"I am not old enough yet to say what they have done to me." That is what she said to me. "You are not old enough to say either," and that is what she also said to me. I hear what they tell her are just stories, stories like the spirit who clawed at the farmer's thatched roof.

When they tell the stories, she sits on their laps, so that the one who is talking is the one who has her on his lap, as if he could not tell the story unless she was on him, and the smoke from their pipes goes right into her hair, and later she smells the same way they smell.

Out back we were leveling the ground and they watched us. She had the rake and I had the pitchfork and we went in circles that way, me pitching the dirt and she raking the stones that came up.

"There is going to be coffee here," they said, and "when it was ready," they said, we "would be old enough to drink it."

They all stood there, their arms crossed and standing in their robes, and I could not help but look at them looking at us, or it was her, they were looking at her, and she looked down at her leg, and there was blood on her leg, and I looked at the pitchfork and I wanted to see if there was blood on one of the ends of the pitchfork, to see if it was the pitchfork I was using that had actually done it.

Then she screamed.

But they did not come running over.

They just stood there and looked at her.

There was a hole in her leg. There was not much blood. That is when I thought that it was not the blood that had made her scream but that it was the stuff showing through the hole in her leg that made her scream.

I took her in and I washed it away. There was dirt there also. It had been on the point on the end of the pitchfork. "Dirt that could have grown the coffee," she said, and took the dirt from the cut and saved it, and the dirt had gotten to be like a little ball because of the blood and the fat it had touched and that it had on it, and she said she was going to take it out back there to the crop and throw it in with the rest of the dirt.

Because she limped, they would sometimes walk next to her and hold her by the arm, or they would make their arms into chairs again and carry her over the field to where we had to go. When she got her hair cut, they would sit her on their laps and put a bowl on her head, and cut with a knife around the bowl from where her hair came out from underneath the bowl. Because the knife shone in the windows at night when they cut, they told her fireflies lived in her hair and that they flew to her pillow to lie and wait for her there until she was done. Once, after her hair was cut, she still wore the bowl on her head, and because all the hair had been cut that came out from underneath the bowl, it looked to me as if her hair was the bowl and that it was moving from side to side when she walked.

They came up around her and they knocked on the bowl. After they knocked on it, she asked them to stop. But they would not stop.

So she sat down in the kitchen, on the floor, and they all came up around her, wearing their robes, and I could not see her anymore, and I could not hear them anymore knocking the bowl that she wore on top of her head, and I called to her, but she did not answer, and then one of them came over and he picked me up and he took me back to my room and locked me in it.

"That was the night I slept in her bed. I thought I was sleeping with the fireflies. When she came in, I did not at first know that it was her because of how short her hair had been cut, and this was the first time that I was seeing it with the bowl taken off.

She went into her bed and she lay down next to me. She said how once she could not fall asleep because every time she started to fall asleep she would hear a flute and she did not know where the flute was, and she woke up and sat up and the flute would stop, and then when she lay back down again it would do it again and so on.

She took my hand and put it down on her, down where it was warm and where it felt to me as if it was the inside of her mouth, or maybe the inside of the cut I had given her with the pitchfork. She said she wished it was her birthday, or she wished I knew the whole story of the spirit who clawed in through the farmer's roof because she wanted to hear my voice saying things. She asked to sit in my lap, and I told her that I did not know any stories, just the one of us in this house with them in their robes and their pipes and us out in the field and them standing with their arms crossed, watching us watch her.

THE FISH KEEPER

W hen my mother said that the Salvation Army was marching through our house, coming to take her away, we took her away. The children and John go to visit her, they go late in the day when there are people up and down the street, I know because I lean out the window and watch the people.

Joshey is twelve years old but now only as tall as some little thing, some tadpole, and bald from the treatments they say he takes. He comes slinking down the street, breaking off car antennas. I almost yell down to him to stop, but I don't want him looking up here at me, and, besides, this child won't be with us much longer and it is not our car he is fooling with.

I make the tuna-in-the-blanket dish for them when they come back from seeing my mother. I like the idea of tucking all that loose flaky tuna into the blanket of dough I've made, then I turn down the sides of the blanket so it looks just like a loaf of bread and not some cookbook surprise.

At night my Matthew cries out for me. I can hear him because his window is open and I'm leaning out of mine so his voice comes from his window, into the street and then up to me. I don't go down to see him because he only cries out once and besides, it is from the street that I hear him crying out and maybe it really isn't Matthew crying out for me but some other kid, that dying Joshey kid crying out for his mother instead.

At times my mother calls me some kind of witch because in my eye I've got what looks like a black pie slice. When I was little I went down in our basement where the floors are dirt and in this city there are not many houses left like this, and I looked at pictures of some others of us, my mother's mother, her mother's mother, women I didn't know, but none of them had this thing in their eye the way I have this thing in my eye, or maybe the pictures were just too old, with the earth of this city covering them up and clouding all the women's faces.

I take my dogs out early when the streets are quiet and you can hear water slapping up against pier pilings at the river. The last time I was in the river I was so young. Then the river was clean and I swam in it. An uncle took me there and held down his hand to pull me up out of the water when I was done with my swim and my body was shaking from the cold. My Rebecca hates this story because she says now the river is just a sea of rubbers shed off from the men the whores get down there.

John is not home again. I am watching the coffee table we have that has the fish tank for its base. My Jack Dempsey feeds like a shark and chases out angels and convicts. I think about how if the fish don't like me looking at them with the pie slice in my eye, then they have nowhere to go, just around and around, and I sit on my couch in my living room and I watch them all I want. "Who has the food?" I say and I shake their can of fish food in the air in circles above their water world.

When I am out with the dogs, I never see anyone, like I said. It's just the sound of the water coming at me from down the street.

I look at John, ask him if he's seen the extra fish tank. I've got to separate this Jack Dempsey from the others. He's eating all their food, even the green terrors' food. I ask John if he hasn't seen the extra fish tank in the bathroom closet, and then I ask him to go look down there to see if it isn't hidden back behind some junk. There is a stack of magazines down there where on the pages the tits of the women are scratched.

"Your mother doesn't talk about the Salvation Army anymore," John says. "She begs to be told of the nurse's vision, "S'il vous plait,' she says to the nurse, 'Tell me the dream,'" and the nurse says, 'Carino, I know not what you are saying.'"

"My baby was bit by a rat," the mother tells me from down below. "This happened in her sleep," she says, "Can you hear me?" she says with a cupped hand above her eyes to shade them from the sun. "It happened in her sleep - how was I to know, we were all asleep," the mother says. "Rat poison's out," she says, "it's all over, they put it in here," she says, "in the trees," she says and she points to the squares of earth on our block with trees growing out of them and ankle-high metal fences around them to keep the earth in. "Rat playgrounds," she says and pets her baby's head.

Leaning out, I see my mother walking down the street wearing her robe and heading for our door. From the pocket of her robe she pulls out her set of keys, and when I go to the stairs I can hear her walking up to them. Before she can get to the top of them, I go down to her and take her to the bathroom where she sits on the side of the tub and says how cold it is. My mother closes her robe tighter around her. With her hair not brushed for what must be many days, it looks like the fuzzy hair on the head of a baby monkey. I take my mother upstairs and sit her down on the couch, where we watch the Jack Dempsey off by himself in his own tank swimming around, headed for corners as if by way of them he will hit upon a door. I let my mother feed the green terrors and the angels, and the convicts, but I am the one to feed the Jack Dempsey.

Before my mother goes away again, I wrap up the slices of the tuna blanket and put them into the pocket of her robe. Looking out the window and down at her on the street, I see that I did not brush her hair and that she has no shoes on her feet.

Even though it is so dirty and teeming with rubbers, little Joshey has taken a dive in the river. "He's yellow," his mother says up to me. "That disease from dirty water, I told him what it is but he thinks it's called Joshness instead. The kid thinks he is a disease. What else could happen to my boy?" the mother says.

One of my dogs eats the rat poison off the street. The Jack Dempsey is floating on his back, rolling over every once in a while like a fat man in the water. I go into the bathroom and sit on the tub. But it is too cold so I go downstairs into the basement we have that still has a dirt floor.

Up above it becomes so loud. I can hear them walking across the floor, the children in their rooms. My mother was right - it sounds like some kind of army marching through this house.

Then I go to the river and jump in and think of all the people out there could be to come and tell me that now I have to get out.

PAN, PAN, PAN

We came in after the crash. We had traveled all night on a ferry boat to arrive. I had slept in a berth with my son, holding him close. When we arrived there were people staring into the ocean. They were looking down at what was floating there in the brackish water of the Nova Scotia shore.

"Look, a toothbrush," my son said and leaned over the pier and pointed. I looked in and it was a toothbrush floating right next to a piling of the pier. I pulled my son back, he was not a swimmer. I did not want him falling in.

Outside the ferry office there were reporters and people with cameras and overhead were helicopters that hovered so close I had thoughts of our hair being shorn by their blades.

My husband and his brother asked what had happened. It was a plane headed for Geneva. It could have been a fire on board. But no one knew for sure. Everywhere the air was filled with the smell of jet fuel.

Traffic was light. No one was driving away from the site. We traveled inland for our holiday. We drove to an inn on a dark lake. It was the geology here, my husband's brother said, that made the lake smell like sulfur, that made the water black like sludge. We stayed in a cabin. The cabin had two bedrooms that shared a wall. It was a short wall that did not reach up to the ceiling. Our son did not want to sleep with us. He wanted to stay with my husband's brother and sleep with him in his bed. At night I would say good-night to my son, my voice carrying over the wall.

There was a fireplace and three rocking chairs in the cabin and we sat in them in the evening. My son sat on my husband's brother's lap while my son held his teddy bear and tore out small bits of its fur and rolled them between his fingers. The teddy bear's face and belly and back were almost all bald from my son doing this.

There was talk of the crash in the dining hall. There were no survivors. The scene was still being combed. Clothes were found floating in the water or washed up and spread out on the rocks as if someone had been doing laundry there and left their things to dry. After dinner, my husband and his brother and my son stood in the office of the inn and watched the News on the television bolted up high on a shelf above the front desk.

I went outside to the lawn, where there was a game of croquet being played in the dusk by the other guests. I slapped mosquitoes landing on my arms and legs and listened to the brightly colored balls gently tapping against one another.

During the day, my husband's brother, who had picked out the inn as our vacation destination and had told us months before how lovely it was, insisted on a swim in the dark lake. He walked out to the end of the dock in front of our cabin and lifted one leg in a jackknife and jumped. But when he jumped, he did not land in deep water. The water came up only to the waist of his shorts and it poured off his big chest and shoulders in dark streams like black blood when he stood up. "It's a good thing I didn't take a dive," he said. "Come on in," he then said. "The water's fine." But my husband and I shook our heads. We could smell the sulfur from where we stood on the end of the dock watching him.

In the dark lake there were dead black trees that were still standing and poking up from the surface of the water. The trees had no tops and the limbs on the trees were broken and the trees looked like one-railed ladders with rungs that spiraled out in all directions going up to the sky. During the day crows sat on the broken limbs from time to time.

There was a boat and my husband and his brother took it out one night while I stayed by the window with my son on my lap. I could hear the oars going through the water and I could hear their voices even after they had been gone a long while.

When they came back it was my turn to go in the boat. I did not want to go. I did not want to leave my son. "Come on," my husband said. "It's beautiful," he said and he made me hand over my son to my husband's brother and I climbed into the boat with my husband. My husband rowed us away from the cabin and I could see my husband's brother and my son on his lap sitting by the window. I could see them because there was a light on in the cabin and I could see my husband's brother leaning over my son and burying his head in my son's belly, making my son laugh. I could hear my son laughing all over the dark lake.

"Stop," I said at one point to my husband. So he stopped rowing, so I could listen, making sure it was really the laughter of my son and not him crying, the two sounding almost the same.

The lake was like many lakes that were connected. My husband would have the boat pass through narrow stretches and then the narrow stretches would give way to large pools, rimmed by the trees with no tops and whose limbs were broken. We heard an owl and we looked for it but we could not see it. We only saw its shape when it took flight and sailed across our heads and then I could hear the flapping of its wings so well I thought how it sounded as if the owl was flapping close enough to me to graze my head with its feet or to touch me lightly with the tips of its wings.

It turned out I knew two people who had died on that plane. Really it was just one I knew. I had been to college with her. She had lived in the dorm room next door. The first few years of college she was overweight. Then she decided to eat only grains and vegetables. She once turned her hand over and showed us her fingers. "They are orange from my love affair with carrots," she had said. She became thin and boys who were once just her friend confessed they now wanted more.

The other person was not someone I had once met. It was by chance we bought a house in Vermont that he summered in as a child with his family. When we bought the house we also bought what was left inside of it. Inside there was some furniture and dishes and some clothes. On hangers were the coats he wore on chilly days and in closets were the fins and masks he had worn while swimming in the pond. In sweaters were labels the mother must have sewn, his name still there. "Paul Hammond". And, then, from his early days as a doctor there was a white coat hanging on a hanger and in blue thread sewn by machine was the name stitched in cursive - "*Dr. Hammond*".

Some guests, who had just arrived from the site of the crash, came into the dining hall. They said they thought they could still smell the jet fuel and so they got up and closed the windows. I could not smell it. All that I could smell was the dark lake. "Smell," they said and held out their arms so I could sniff their shirt sleeves. "Fuel," they said.

"Why are there so many little pieces?" my son wanted to know about the parts of the plane the recovery crew was bringing up onto the rocky shore. My husband explained to my son how water can be as hard as a sidewalk if you crash into it fast enough. My son sucked his thumb and listened to the news report. Apparently, the crew had radioed the tower. "Pan-pan," they had said, using the international urgency call before it became a full-fledged May-Day.

My son liked saying it. "Pan, Pan, Pan," he said on a walk in the woods. He did not want to walk with me and hold my hand. He wanted to be on my husband's brother's shoulders where my husband's brother carried him up high and ducked down low when tree branches were in the way.

"Pan, Pan, Pan," he said lying on a log, looking down into a stream at leaves he had placed in the water to watch them race in the current, while I worried he might slide off the log and be swept away in the current.

On the walk back to the inn my boy said, "Shh, listen" and we stopped. It was a mockingbird calling, its song repeated three times. "Even he is saying *pan, pan, pan*," my boy said pointing at the mockingbird sitting on a branch.

The girl I knew from college was flying to Geneva to meet her fiancée. From there they would fly to France to see her sister. Her sister was about to have a baby, and the girl I knew was going to visit her and help with the baby. The girl and her sister were best friends, I remember because the sister had also gone to my college and the two of them were always together. I would sometimes study with them in a room in our library called the roost because it was a loft built up high on a platform with railings on all sides. It looked like a tree house. We would study and talk and drink Tab and eat Snickers bars sometimes in the roost. This was before my friend became a vegetarian and before her love affair with carrots. But the roost was not the place to really get work done, it was the place to go if you wanted to talk and to laugh and that is what the three of us mostly did there.

At night, over the short wall, we talked to my husband's brother and my son. One night my husband's brother told us about his grown daughter and we listened to how she was interested in cooking now. He described a holiday meal she had made for him. The cranberry sauce was made with tangerine and cherries. The duck was glazed in honey. After a while, everyone was quiet and I could hear them snoring but I was wide awake. It was a hot, still night and I was too hot to sleep. I walked out of the cabin and onto the dock. Maybe my husband's brother was right. Maybe the water was just fine. I took off my clothes and jumped in. The water felt as warm as the air. For a second, when I came up I was not sure I was even out of the water. Then I felt the water rolling off me, off my hair and body and falling back into the water and I knew I was up out of the water and I could breathe.

It was standing there in the water up to my waist when I thought I heard my son yelling, "Pan, Pan, Pan" again and so I got out of the water and ran back to the house to see why he was awake. Maybe he had dreamt a bad dream. The fire in the fire-place was just embers now and as I walked through the door, the little breeze I made stoked the embers and made them glow a deep red. My husband's brother was already standing in the doorway of their room. He was expecting me. His large body took up the door frame and I could not see around him. I could not see my son. "He's fine," my husband's brother said. "He must have had a bad dream. He's back asleep now," he said. I nodded and then my husband's brother said good-night and closed their door. I dried off and climbed into bed next to my husband who was still sleeping. I could smell the sulfur smell of the dark lake that I had brought into the bed with me. I could not fall asleep for the longest time. The smell was keeping me awake. I tried to listen for the sound of my son breathing, but the sound of my husband and his brother snoring was much too loud. I could not hear him over the wall.

The News we saw on the television said that Dr. Paul Hammond was on the plane to go to a meeting in Geneva. The News called him a pioneer in the battle against aids. My husband had told my son about pioneers once, about how they had traveled in covered wagons across the country, about how they had eaten hard tack and used their wagons to float across rivers. My son wanted to know why if this man was a pioneer, he did not use the plane like a covered wagon, and float in it across the sea to the safety of shore.

In the dining hall one morning, my husband's brother put down his foot. There would be no more talk of the crash. Not on his vacation. Everyone in the dining hall was talking about it and it wasn't what we had come to this place for. We had not come to stay in an inn with braided rugs on the floors, that had breakfasts of maple syrup and blueberry pancakes, that had rockers on a wide wooden porch, that had trails through tall pines to talk of wreckage all day. It's not good for your son, my husband's brother said to me, to hear this kind of talk. It gives him nightmares. We were quiet at the table then. We sipped our tea. We looked around the room. A guest at a table next to ours held his hand out like a plane flying over the water, then he nose-dived his hand and had it crash into the daisy patterned table-cloth that covered the table. It was obvious he was describing the crash to the others who sat at the table with him. "This will all die down soon, my husband said. People will forget the crash," he said.

That night my husband's brother and my son said they wanted take a walk. "Maybe," my husband's brother told my son, "we will come upon a bear," and my husband's brother raised his huge shoulders up and held out his hands like claws and growled above my laughing son.

My husband said to me, "While they're on a walk we can take the boat out on the lake."

"Do you think there are bears here?" I asked my husband while he rowed us on the dark lake. I was nervous for my boy.

"Don't be silly," my husband said.

It was a windy night and my husband said that he could smell autumn in the air. I could only smell the dark lake, its smell seemed stronger than ever, as if the wind rippling the surface peeled back a layer of smell that was even stronger than the first layer. "How can you smell anything but the lake?" I said. I wrinkled up my nose.

"It doesn't smell to me," my husband said.

"I cannot sleep because of the smell," I said.

"Oh, come on," my husband said. "This is a beautiful lake," he said, he motioned with his arms at the broken trees surrounding us.

When we got back to shore my husband's brother was running around the house. He was banging open the doors to our rooms. He was looking for our son. "We were on a walk," he said out of breath. "And then he disappeared. I thought he came back here." We looked too. I called his name. There was no answer. My husband even looked up the chimney and called his name up there. "The lake!" I yelled. I ran outside and I jumped off the dock. I landed in the shallow water that would have been too deep for my son who was not a swimmer. I could not see. There was no way that I could see. I thrashed my arms through the water. I tried to feel if he was there. On land I could hear my husband and his brother still calling out his name. He had not been found. What had my husband's brother done to my boy?

I ran through the water, but that was hard to do. I slogged through it really in my heavy denim jeans. I screamed his name. I kicked beneath me to somehow dredge him up. There were layers to the lake, I already knew. I dove in and dug through the dirt. On the surface, taking a breath of air and looking quickly on the shore for him, something swooped over my head. It was just an owl, but for a moment I thought it was my son. He was all right. He had grown wings. He was safe. Was that how it now was for the families of the victims of the crash? Were they busy too with thoughts of their loved ones taking other forms? Were there some seagulls in the air who were once men and women from the fatal flight? The owl hooted and headed for the tree lined shore. Then I noticed that the water did not seem to smell of sulfur. The smell had changed. Jet fuel, I thought. The smell so strong the crash could have been right here in this shallow dark lake and not out on the ocean far away. That is when I ran out of the water. I ran dripping, the water from the black lake falling off me as I went all the way across the road past the other cabins and to the lawn where the croquet balls were lying all in the same dark shapes, the bright colors they were in daylight now impossible to see.

He was perched on the front desk. Sitting cross-legged over the sign-in book for the guests, his eyes on the television screen reporting the late news. He did not turn his head to look at me when I called his name. "Oh, Mama," he said. "You've got to see this."

We could not stay. I was dripping the black lake water all over the braided office rug. "It stains," the front desk person said, asking me to kindly leave. I picked my son up and carried him back to our cabin with my head near his, and I smelled his hair the whole way and I kept smelling it even in bed with him that night and I thought why hadn't I done this all along, just smelled his hair? It would have kept me from smelling the lake.

My son wanted to sleep with me because my husband and his brother were already asleep and he wanted to whisper in my ear. He didn't want to wake them and he didn't want my husband's brother hearing what he had to say about the crash that he had learned on the News. He didn't want my husband's brother to tell him to stop talking about it.

He rattled off facts. 229 people were aboard. The plane shattered into a million pieces. There was a fire on the plane. It could have been from a wire. There are 150 miles of wire inside a plane. There are no smoke alarms inside the ceiling of a plane. If planes were restaurants they would not pass the safety codes, they would not get an occupancy permit. The frame of a plane is called a jig. "Did you know that, Mama?" I did not.

"I bet it looked just like a silver bird on fire," my son said.

My son held his bear in the dark and I knew he was rolling bits of his bear's fur between his fingers while he talked. "What else?" I said to my son. "Tell me more."

"There were no bodies, just parts. A woman had a funeral for her daughter with no body," my son whispered in my ear. I liked hearing what my son had to say. I was thankful for the crash. It drowned out the sound of my husband and his brother snoring. It helped me forget about the smell off the dark lake. It gave me back my son.

A few years after the crash, in our house, in the house Doctor Paul Hammond had summered in as a child, we tried to make room for more things. We put the old clothes that were in the house when we bought the house in boxes. We were planning on a trip to the goodwill. I lifted the white lab coat with Dr. Hammond's name on it that was hanging on a hanger where it had hung for years. When I lifted it off my son said, "Look, ladybirds," and I looked down and saw that ladybugs had started falling out from inside the sleeves.

"Ladybugs," I said, correcting my son while I lifted the collar of the coat. There were ladybugs in there too. There were ladybugs all over in the coat. Some flew and some landed on the floor when I shook the coat. There must have been close to a hundred. The coat was alive with them.

"Ladybird, ladybird, fly away home, your house is on fire. And your children will burn," my son said while looking closely at one that had landed on his finger.

I did not send off the coat with the other clothes for the goodwill. Instead, I left the coat hanging on its hanger in our house. It's still there now, among our winter clothes.

LESTER

*C*ome in here and I got to lay the cardboard shit out and tape it down. It don't stay down. It gets dirty. It gets a hole in it. Coming and coming like this place, fucking Barbados. This ain't no Barbados. Someone slips, breaks their neck. I get the heat, man.

What you reading?

Stars, man, my daddy knew about stars. He died looking at one. The Big Zipper. "Hold still," he said, "just look up." We were on top the house. I looked up. But then I saw my daddy looking down, and I thought I had to look down too, like there were stars down on the street I didn't know about. When Daddy died, Redmond, that's my brother, he said Daddy died looking at the stars. "He died from it," Redmond said.

I go up to the top of our house and I look down. You know what I see? Some sweater on the ground, some sweater looks like it was killed, the arms all spread out. Like maybe the sweater jumped from our fucking roof. Maybe that's what killed my daddy, looking at the sweater. Like made him want to fit into that sweater and be dead.

I can't ever find the fucking Big Zipper. I look up. I say to Redmond, "Where is it? I can't find it." Redmond says he's got the moon. He says it's easy to find the moon. But we can't ever find the Big Zipper. I look down. I see the sweater, the fucking street. There ain't nothing on our street. Sure, there's something on our street, but it ain't nothing. It's the street, man - what's to tell about a fucking street?

Here they come, more of them. Up goes my cardboard like some broken shit, like some broken cardboard. Hector comes over. He whispers in my fucking ear he can hear El Dios. He can hear El Dios when the fucking bus goes by. My boss, he comes over, and my boss says, "Dios Mio, I told you to be putting some cardboard down. You want somebody to come in here and break their stupid coño neck - do you, Lester, their coño neck?"

I get the heat. Breaking down the cardboard boxes, cutting tape and taping this shit to the fucking wet-ass floor.

I ain't never been to Barbados. I ain't never seen no palm tree. Hector has heard El Dios in the palm trees. "Tio, they be shaking in the wind - it's his whisper in your ear, man."

Murphy, you ever been to Barbados? I ain't never seen no palm tree. Hector has heard El Dios in the palm trees. "Tio, they be shaking in the wind - it's the whisper in your ear, man."

Murphy, you ever been to Barbados?

No, uh-huh.

Fucking Hector, he think he hear El Dios when the bus goes by.

"Lester," my mama says, "sit me at the window."

The fucking street is full of shit. Summer and the water goes by and the shit sticks on the street. You ever seen such a street? That shit don't want to go nowheres. I get up on top of the house and I look down and I yell at that shit. Me and

Redmond yell. The way we see it, it's a free ride to somewheres. "Rego Park!" Redmond yells, and he points, he knows which way it is. "Barbados," I'm yelling. I'm pointing for the shit sticked to the fucking street. Then the bus goes by and me and Redmond look at each other. With the bus going by, this house shakes.

"Lester," Mama says, "take me back to my bed."

I be singing and Hector puts a hand on me. "I talk to him too," he says, "and you know what? He answer me."

Stars be what my daddy died of, Redmond tells us Easter. Being Redmond, he does Grace. Mama, her hand all shaking, puts pork on a plate for Daddy, even though Daddy been so dead now.

I ride the bus.

Murphy, I seen you ride the bus.

I get the heat. Break your fucking coño necks. Coño, coño, coño. The bus going by and I open up the fucking coño doors and yell at it some more coño. Coño all the way to Rego Park. Coming and coming in here with the fucking snow. My fucking cardboard. Murphy, what are you doing? What you want to know stars for? I'll tell you about stars. The Big Zipper you can't ever find. Stars with animal names, forget it, whatever named them stars wasn't thinking. Whatever named stars, bear, and bull and shit, he was looking out his window, he was living in the woods, he was looking down off the top of his house see-ing wild animals running around. What you want to know about stars for? Little Zipper, you can't ever find that. You can't find the Big Zipper, then forget about the little one. Redmond, he's just like you, he's got a magazine page with the stars all on them. He goes up to the top of our house and compares. There ain't nothing on the page like there is up there. There ain't nothin. Down below, man, you got the street, you got the dead sweater, you got the shit sticked on - it ain't going to let go.

Leaving, man, shit, now they're leaving. Leaving and leav-ing and stepping right back over my wet-ass floor. Murphy, hear the bus? Fucking world's cracking open when it go by. The lights on my street, man, shaking off and on - hey, daytime, hey, nighttime!

Fucking lights having a good time. Mama says, "Child Lester child, child Redmond Child, we going to have supper," Mama says.

North Star, fuck, I can't even see Bensonhurst from up top my house. But my daddy always said, "North Star, Lester, that's the easiest one. That's the one you got to know." Meantime, fucking sweater on the street gets run over and over again, arms crossed, arms out, died this way, died that way, can't make up its fucking coño sweater head.

Fuck Barbados. Man, I could fuck it. Get on down in Barbados. Fuck the palm trees. Fuck the water. Man, I want to fuck it. I could fuck Rego Park first. Bam, I could fuck Co-Op City. Bam, I could move on down. Fuck Newark. Bam, fuck the Carolinas. Fuck the Keys. Murphy, I don't fuck much. "Lester," Daddy said to me, "Don't fuck too much." I don't fuck too much. Fucking stars, what you want to know about stars for? "Mama," I say, "Mama whose sweater is that?" Mama, at the window, looks down. "Ain't Redmond's," Mama says.

You see this cardboard, man? Murphy, man. This ain't cardboard no more. This be like other than cardboard. This be like I don't know what. This be like something ain't nothing. Redmond's buying shit to look through. Says with it now he sees things real close. Puts it to his eye and shakes his head. Says he sees all of what Daddy sees.

Coño - my cardboard. Ain't El Dios here. No El Dios flapping his mouth under my cardboard. Tell it to Hector. Lester says ain't no El Dios. Says, no palm trees here. Some clankety-clank bus coming on down the street. My boss saying I got to lay it down, saying, "Lester, what you want? Some stupid coño necks breaking all over the place? Lester?"

What I want, Murphy? I don't want it saying Lester no more. You can hear it through the windows. Whole street be cooking something in a fry pan. All the grease popping, saying my name, the longest Lester name, saying - Lessssssssssssssssster.

THE ONLY LIGHT TO SEE BY

*T*he girl was trying to show her mother how the people down the road were found dead. The girl lay every which way on the sheets with the American Eagles all over them, saying, "This is how the daughter was found dead, and this is how the father was found dead, and this is how the mother was found dead."

The girl's mother lifted up the covers and covered the girl with them, making the bed as if the girl were not there, the mother thought to herself, as if the girl were just another American Eagle on the sheets.

The girl wanted to go down the road to the house. At first, the mother told the girl that she could not go, but then the mother told her that if it was something the girl wanted to see, then the mother would go with the girl, and the mother thought that seeing the house where the family was actually killed might stop the girl from every once in a while, while they were eating dinner or watching television, might stop the girl from lying out on the floor in the way one of the bodies was found and saying to her mother, "Guess who I am now, the father or the daughter or the mother?"

It was raining when they walked down to the house. Worms had come out from the dirt on the sides of the road and the worms stuck to the bottom of their shoes, and the girl told her mother that she had learned that you can cut a worm in half and it will still crawl.

Walking behind her mother, the girl told her mother that the back of her mother's head, where no hair grows and leaves a circle of skin, that the back of her mother's head was the moon and that the long hair that still grew down from the sides of the moon was the night.

The girl led the way to the house. She counted the worms she killed under her shoes, saying, "Two, four, six, eight," counting double because she said she knew that when you cut a worm in half that both ends will live.

First thing the girl said to her mother was that it looked like their house. That, from the outside, the girl said, it looked as though people had lived in there. Then the mother and the girl saw a dog on the porch and the girl said, "It must be the family dog, come back to the house to sit and wait for the family to come home."

The mother and the girl stood outside the ropes that circled around the house, and the girl said to her mother that it was as if they were watching a parade and the house was a float that had lost its air and now could not float any longer and had to come down to the ground.

The girl told her mother that she wanted to come back to the house after the rope was gone or that she wanted to come back when it was night.

The mother took the girl back home. When the mother went to bed that night, the girl stood up on her mother's bed and wrapped the covers around herself like a cape, and the mother thought to herself that the girl looked as if she were an eagle, grown from out of the sheets and ready to fly.

In the middle of the night, the girl was gone. The mother walked down the road and called for the girl, but the mother heard no answer. When the mother reached the house where the bodies had been found dead, she went under the ropes and into the house.

The television was on and it was the only light to see by in the house. There was what the mother thought was dried blood on the floor by the couch, but because it seemed to be such a dark color in the television light, the mother thought it could have been anything on the floor and that it could have even been water.

Then the mother saw the girl lying on the couch, one arm up over her head, fitting into the line of chalk that had been drawn to show how the daughter had lain when the daughter had been killed.

The mother called to the girl, but the girl was asleep. Then the mother sat down next to the girl and put the girl's feet up on her lap, and the mother looked around the room. By the wall she saw the chalk lines where the father had lain when he had been killed. The mother looked for the other mother's place where she had been killed, but she could not find the lines of chalk. Then the mother put her arms on the couch and she saw that where she was sitting there was an outline drawn in chalk of someone who had long hair, and the hair had gone over the back of the couch, and the mother thought to herself that what it looked like was a flame reaching down to the ground, and the mother then thought that it was where she was sitting that the other mother had sat when the mother had been killed.

The girl woke up and looked at the back of her mother's head, and the girl told her mother that she thought that it was the back of her mother's head that was lighting up the room at first, and not the light from the television. "I thought the moon was in the house," the girl said to her mother, and then the mother lifted up the girl and carried her home.

At home, the mother put the girl into the mother's own bed, with the eagles on the sheets, and the girl lay down and slept as if what she was trying to do was fit into one of the eagles, spreading her arms out like wings, and then the mother got into bed and lay on top of the girl, so that the back of the mother's head, with the circle of skin with the hair hanging down from its sides was facing up and looked like the moon, and the mother thought that if they were both to be killed in their sleep, she and the girl would be found as one, the mother on top of the daughter in a circle of light.

THE BEAUTY IN BULLS

"*O*h, my badness."

"Oh, your badness what?"

"This is a thoroughly bodacious ta-ta business."

"Here, look at this one."

"Oh, and a bodacious walk, bodacious hair, bodacious legs, bodacious badness."

"This is the one where they take him away by horse and cart."

"I bet she's been tupped just now.   She has that look of just having been tupped."

"She is not a ewe."

"Hey, why did God create women?"

"There are twenty-six in all - and see, this is the one beforehand, when he is alive and well and in the field."

"I want to come in her hair."

"They say the meat is given to orphans."

"Did you just hear what I said?"

"You want to come in her hair. This is the one where the picadores come out. My God, he almost looks ready for it. Look how he is bending his head low and revealing that neck. That neck of his looks so strong. That neck looks so strong that it looks like there is a man inside of it."

"There is a man inside of my badness."

"Then comes the cape trick."

"Then comes the cape trick."

"Do you remember it?"

"Her ta-tas are the size of teacups."

"There is a roar in the crowd."

"She is a walking hutchful of delicate cups and saucers and bowls."

"I want to open her glass doors and take down her china."

"You never saw anything so red."

"I want to bring a cup up to my mouth and suck on it so hard that it stays there because of my suck. You know the suck you had when you were a kid? Afterward, I am going to show her the rim it made around my mouth."

"It is a horrible thing to see such a big animal hurt by his own size when he falls on himself. It is just one more thing to happen to him."

"The cup still feels like it is there later, around your mouth."

"Do you think Picasso knew this?"

"Your lips look as if they were in some kind of kissing derby for the last ten days."

"I keep looking at these lines he has drawn. After a while, it looks to me as if the man with their capes could be the bulls, and the bulls rearing, they could be the men. Is that all Picasso or is that me?"

"Her legs are like candles."

"Jesus, horns."

"I bet you want to ask me which are the tapered ends."

"He has even drawn in the men and the women holding up their white handkerchiefs."

"The ends with the wicks."

"When they could not wave handkerchiefs, they waved anything. They waved cigarette packs."

"Well, I haven't decided yet. Go suck on a candle. A long thin candle."

"Beer cans."

"Well, it is bodacious."

"Let me count. Six men on foot, three on horseback."

"It is like sucking on her finger."

"Here he has turned around as if to say how dare you. This is the how-dare-you look. This is the look when the men run behind the little wooden walls. This is when the crowd stands up and cheers for the bull."

"Her eyes are rocks in the water."

"This is when people want to see the man die because there is always that possibility and they want to see it happen. They have paid to come in. They want to see it."

"Have you ever pulled the most beautiful rock out of the ocean and put it on your dresser and the next day you look at the rock and you think how you could have ever thought that that rock was beautiful, because now it is so white and dry it is not a rock but a bone?"

"In the end, I would rather take the side of the bull. I would rather see the bull win. He is the stronger of the two. The crowd has paid, but maybe now they forget that that matters, maybe now they are just thinking that they don't even want to look at the man because the man is so weak and they are so embarrassed by the man."

"I will never suck her eyes out."

"They all want to be bulls now."

"The crowd, all of them in the crowd, want to be bulls."

"To have them go white on my dresser top."

"And when the man wins, when the bull is stuck, they are

so relieved. They never did want to be bulls. Who knows what a bull does, anyway? they say. Let the man win, they say. Up go the handkerchiefs."

"Can you hear it when he's stuck?"

"It is like sticking a knife into meat and pulling it out. It goes thwack."

"Thwack?"

"If they are good, then the ears go; if they are really good, then also goes the tail."

"I have tried to put those rocks back into tap water. But it does no good."

"The women want the ears. The women want the tails. Whatever do they do with them? It is enough to imagine that all the beautiful women could possibly be living in houses with trunkfuls of bull ears and bull tails. Because only the beautiful women are given the ears and the tails."

"Maybe it is why God created beautiful women."

"This is my favorite one. See how the man is down on one knee in front of the bull and the cape, too, is down on the ground? This shows the bull is ready, this shows the bull could if he wanted to."

"Maybe I am confusing things here, maybe she has never ever been tupped before. Maybe this is what my bodacious badness is picking up."

"She is not a ewe."

"I want to be her first."

"I respect the banderilleros."

"There would be a world opened unto her."

"In this one, they sit in a chair and wait for the bull. The bull's tail is saying, 'What are you doing? Don't you know?'"

"She will remember me for the rest of her life. And it is not an only-girl thing, it is anyone's thing. I remember my first. Everyone remembers their first. Really everyone's first is not unmemorable. Or maybe I mean everyone's first is barely memorable, because what is bigger in all the world at that moment is that you are doing it. Here is where it all falls apart. Here is where I really do wonder do I want to be her first?"

"Salto con la garrocha, jump with the javelin."

"But how will I know I will be her first unless I am her first? There is no way to tell. Over dinner, over coffee."

"Echar perros al toro, thrown to the dogs."

"But she will tell me just before I am about to begin to suck on her cups."

"Picasso is my hero."

"If I am her first or eighty-first."

"Oh, eighty-one, that's a lot."

"For anyone's ta-tas"

"When you get to number forty, you are already in the bodacious zone."

"Shh, I am thinking."

"This bull's thing is big. This thing is monstrous. This bull makes me feel stumpy. Outdone by a bull. Next thing you know, she will be wanting this bull."

"I remember being there and wanting a drink because of the sight of the blood. But then I became used to it and I watched, and at the end, when they dragged the bull around and he became dirty on his back. I liked it."

"If your first is a bull, then are you part bull the rest of your life? Does it make her, then, a cow? I cannot believe she stooped to do it with a bull. Oh, she is some cow."

"How many bulls a day?"

"Will that bull suck on her cups?"

"Imagine, all the orphans. Oh no, not bull again! they say at the table."

"When he is done with her, that bull, he will take her eyes out with his horns."

"Bull soup."

"Let me at that bull."

"My aunt has been invited to dinner, and Rey Juan Carlos will be there."

"Oh?"

"My aunt can't believe they are serving quenelles cooked in Madeira and amontillado."

"That bodacious Rey Juan Carlos."

"Oh, to see their faces if the bull soup was served."

"Damn, that bull's thing is big."

"Do you really think he walks around that ring thinking, 'My God, look, everyone, look how really big my thing is?'"

"No."

"He is thinking, 'Why am I here, what can I do?'"

"Why am I here and what can I do?"

"That's right. That is the whole nine yards."

"Tell your aunt to say so at the dinner, then."

"I would have loved to have been a fly on the wall when Picasso was drawing these things."

"How big was Picasso's thing?"

"Did they come to him in a dream?"

"Artists all have small things."

"Say bull tongue over and over again and see what does it sound like."

"I am no artist."

"Botha, Botha, Mr. South Africa."

"Why am I here? What can I do? I have a thing so big."

"Bull is a specialty over there in South Africa."

"I will drown her."

"Bodacious Botha."

"Imagine wanting to do it with a bull. How does she do it? Does she swallow?"

"If you are to be her first, then what will she know from swallowing?"

"She has swallowed it from the bull."

"There is beauty in bulls."

"And not in cows?"

"Picasso did not draw cows."

"He should have. Let me tell you about cows. Cows are

big. It is insane to think that they could never hurt you. But they do not. It makes me think - Is the cow so big to size up with the bull? And only with the bull?

"Let me have a look at that girl."

"Now we both have our bodacious badness on."

"When you get to her, you will not have to think, 'Why am I here and what can I do?'"

"No, I will say, 'Look at me. See the size my thing is. I will do what I must do.'"

KATO AND THE INDIANS
FROM HERE

*I*t was sweet bananas I saw him buy at Bertha's. But with his mouth up into Jolie, I saw I would have to wait a while before I got any. She stood on the chair, and looked like she was ready to pull something down off a shelf, and his mouth was up into her, and it looked like his head was up a pipe and he was looking for something stuck in it.

I could smell the sweet bananas through the brown paper bag. Bertha sold her candy in these bags so tiny that when you carried one out you thought, "I am the size of a doll." That is what I thought when I passed by all her matchbox cars where the boys were standing closing in on the glass case and pointing out the ones they would like to drive.

"Come on," Jolie would say to me and take me by the hand and lead me past the boys and out into the street.

His name was Kato, so it made sense to me then that his mouth was up and open inside of her because his name sounded like it was something always open and that it wouldn't shut until someone came along and shut it for him, which is what Jolie did for him when she said, "Kato, don't." It was a chair from school, the seat splintered and the legs uneven. Jolie teetered while she stood on it and Kato pulled away from her, his mouth red around the rim like his mouth had been on a cherry popsicle and not on my sister.

The whole time he held onto the sweet bananas, or rather they were pushed up under his armpit where I could see his hair sticking out around the brown paper bag. Jolie pulled up her shorts and got down to sitting on the chair. She looked over at me in the doorway and then she took the bag out from Kato's armpit and she threw me the sweet banana. Then she fed Kato a sweet banana and then he fed her the other end and then Jolie said, "Ow, damn," and lifted up her leg from the splintered chair seat and looked at the underside of her leg and passed her hand over it.

Once, while going by those boys at Bertha's, I had stolen dollar bills stuffed into one of their back pockets. I don't think anyone saw me do it and with the dollars I turned around and brought more sweet bananas. Bertha had a beard and I wondered who her husband was when I paid her the money.

Our mother and our father had Indian parties. Me and Jolie would chop the hard boiled eggs and put them into a bowl and we would put the coconut shavings into a bowl and we would put the peanuts and the raisins and the chutney into bowls and the whole house smelled like curry and our mother's fingertips would be stained yellow and her mouth would be stained yellow from when she tasted the food off her wooden spoon.

"Indian," me and Jolie would holler and then hit our mouths and hoot like Indians doing war dances and then our mother would stop us and dot our foreheads with curry sauce, and say, "This is Indian from India." But me and Jolie hooted anyway and jumped on one foot and then the other and tied our dolls around our backs and put a peacock feather in our braids.

What Kato did at night we did not know. From our place we could not see his window. We could see his building, a straight wall without windows and made out of bricks. Sometimes we would go up to the wall and Jolie would place a glass against it and listen to what she said was Kato breathing, Kato sleeping, the creak of Kato's bones.

What Kato did during the day, we did not know either. After school he would meet us at Bertha's and then take Jolie's arm and steer her through the streets and Jolie had me by the arm. The three of us traveled hooked together that way until we got to the street with the park. Once there, Kato let go and Jolie let go of me and I went into the boat that didn't sail because it was cement and built into the ground. I climbed its stacks and looked through its portholes out over the sea of sand. Kato and Jolie would go to the basement of a building, and that is where I found Jolie standing on a chair and Kato with his mouth up under her. The sea of sand had butts from cigarettes in it and when I squinted I would say they looked like small fish showing their backs up through the waves. The others in the boat would squint also and we would watch the fish while the cars on the street circling the park honked their horns and drove by.

The boys with their matchbox cars wheeled them along the side of the boat, and the boy I had stolen money from made sounds like car engines and bubbles of spit came out around his mouth.

"What do Indians from India do?" we asked our mother and she said, "They sit in rooms with arched doorways, cover themselves in gold threaded cloth and tell each other stories of how men became thieves, girls became women, boys became men, women grew old."

Our mother went to her drawer and pulled out cloth from India that was threaded with gold. "Touch this," she said and we did and we lifted the cloth and it was heavy, as heavy as the curtains that covered our windows that faced our street.

"Who could wear this?" we said.

"Brides and mourners, women," our mother said. Some of the gold threads had broken and they were sticking up straight from the cloth.

"Ouch," my sister, Jolie said. "This could hurt."

Our mother brought the cloth to our faces and covered everything but our eyes. We thought we smelled perfume.

"Sandalwood," our mother said, and showed us a bar of soap wrapped in paper decorated with the faces of Indian women.

One morning, Jolie went to our mother's drawer and took the sandalwood soap. On the walk to school, Jolie rubbed the soap behind her ears and down the length of her neck.

"Do the backs of my knees," she said and I did and in the middle of the street we stopped and I took the soap and rubbed it on the backs of her knees and it left a mark the way chalk left a mark on cloth when you were making a pattern and ready to start cutting.

That afternoon, Bertha was not there and a man was there instead.

"Is this her husband?" I thought to myself. This man did not know where anything was in the store. I had to point and show him where the sweet bananas were and the bag he put them in was not the small doll-size bag Bertha would give us, but it was big and the boys who were not pressed up against the glass looking at the matchbox cars were out on the street, blowing up the bags and bursting them with their hands so that the bags made sounds like slamming doors.

Kato carried the bag. He carried it like it held something other than the sweet bananas but something more like groceries, a gallon of milk, canned goods, things that could break through the bottom. He carried it with both arms and walked ahead of me and Jolie down the street. When we got to the park he did not take Jolie to the building where the school chair was, instead he went and sat on one of the stacks from the boat sailing in the sea of sand. Kids looked at him sitting up there and I thought if somebody's mother were here she would come over and tell him to get down, that the boat wasn't for kids with legs as long as his. Once in a while Kato threw us down a sweet banana that would fall in the sand and we would wipe it off on our shirts before eating it.

"What do you see?" Jolie yelled up to Kato. But Kato didn't answer, so me and Jolie looked through the portholes. I pointed out the cigarette butts looking like fish, but Jolie said she couldn't see them and then she turned around and yelled up to Kato, "Hey, it was me who bought those sweet bananas."

I felt like telling her it wasn't she who bought them, that it was me and it was some man, maybe Bertha's husband who sold them to me and that is how I knew, but I didn't say anything. Jolie stood there in the sand, with her hands on her hips, just looking up at Kato. Kato threw down the empty bag and it landed on the sand. Jolie kicked it far and the kid I stole the money from was there and he picked it up and blew the bag up and burst it with his hands.

I ran over to the kid and I kicked him in the shin. The kid ran away and then Jolie started calling Kato a thief. Kato didn't listen and he just put his hand over his eyes as if he were watching other boats sailing by in the distance. I did the same as Kato with my hand over my eyes, but there were only cars to watch and as far down the streets as one could see. Jolie looked down and grabbed my hand from my eyes and then she said, "Come on," and we walked fast out of the park.

On the street I saw the kid again who I stole money from and I looked for something in my school bag to throw at him. I found the bar of sandalwood soap and I threw it and it bounced off his head. It fell under a running sprinkler and started to bubble and the whole park started to smell like sandalwood soap.

Jolie and I started running. We ran all the way out to the piers and then, even on the piers, we were still running, our feet sometimes falling through holes where the wood had rotted through. Rusted cables and bolts as big as car tires tripped us. At the end of the pier we jumped under it and sat down where there was a ledge and a broken sign tacked to a piling that must have once said, "No Fishing," but now said, "No ing." "No nothing," Jolie said. The smell of the river was strong under the ledge where no wind blew threw.

"This is what it's like inside a fish," Jolie said.

That night our mother and father were having an Indian party. Our mother wore her gold threaded cloth like a skirt. Our father sat in a chair and smoked from a pipe. Guests stayed late.

"I am going to the park," Jolie said. Going to the park at night was like going to school at night, it was like going to a movie house in the middle of the day, it was something we never did. "Stay here," Jolie said. So I stayed with the smells of curry and looked at everyone's faces stained yellow and I waited for Jolie to come home.

When she finally came back she went up to my mother and pulled on her gold threaded skirt and said, "Mommy, I've got to tell you something." But our mother did not listen and instead she filled glass bowls with more peanuts. Then Jolie went to our father and said, "Daddy," but she did not finish what she was going to say because our father walked away from her and turned a record over.

In our bed that night Jolie said, "I wanted to tell them how I stood on that chair while that Kato kid put his mouth up between my legs."

In our room there was a light coming from somewhere creating shadows on the wall.

"See that?" Jolie said and pointed to a shadow. "It's an Indian," and she got out of bed and touched the wall where the shadow was. "This is his hatchet. This is not an Indian from India Indian. This is one of us," she said and then Jolie came back to bed and she took her hand and put it to her mouth to make the hooting sound that Indians made and she started hooting like an Indian doing a war dance from her bed, and then I started hooting too, and that is how we both fell asleep, with our hands covering our mouths.

AUNT GERMAINE

*R*ings and necklaces are warm from my aunt's skin when she pulls them up from under her covers and puts them in my hand. How can the body of this old woman still make things warm?

I look at the jewelry. There are faux pearls and gold birds with rhinestones for eyes. A Christmas tree has bulbs of colored glass.

"Where did you get these?" I ask my aunt.

"Places I have been to," she says. "In Egypt," she says, "I bought a box whose lid engravings told the story of the Nile."

"Where is it now?" I ask.

"Here," she says, and she pats her blanket.

"In Amsterdam I bought delft clogs," she says, "on them were painted windmills."

"And from India?" I say.

"From India," she says, and then she does not finish and she falls asleep.

Outside the clouds are not whole but look like they have been skywritten by planes that left puffs of letters that now, after time, can no longer be read. My aunt's breathing sounds like she is whistling through her nose. I take hold of the end of the blanket and very slowly pull it back. All around her there are chocolate wrappers. With one hand in her sleep she holds onto chains made out of gold. By her feet are kid gloves whose long arms are embroidered with climbing vines. On the other side of my aunt there is a beaded purse and silver chopsticks. At her neck there are rings. Between her legs are brass candleholders and a doily and a small postal balance. At the end of the bed there is a tiger's foot, a sock, a man's shoe and the engraved box from Egypt.

"Aunt Germaine, Aunt Germaine," I say.

When she wakes up, she tells me lies, and they are better than your truths. She remembers cars filled with so many roses you could not see to drive. She remembers men so handsome mothers hid from their own husbands, afraid of accusations of infidelity. She remembers boats so long they carried a fleet of taxis for passengers set on going forward and aft. She remembers sleepwalking maids who scaled ceilings at night and dusted daytime. She remembers women who lived on lawns and property because they could not get in the house.

"What about India?" I say.

"Oh, India," she says, "cows that read people's palms - predicted death and children. Foretold gains, stated losses lost, estimated the depth of a lover's love, based fears on the leftward rightward way a middle finger slants." "Sacred as all shit, those cows," my aunt says, and then plucks up a chocolate from under her blanket and wipes her fingers on the pillowcase.

We are somewhere in the nation's capital. I have come here in a car that kept breaking down. I have come here asking for directions along the way. This street we are on has the name of a tree — Sycamore Terrace or Cedar Lane or Walnut Place, it does not matter which. There is an island in the driveway. From this window I can see it. My Aunt Germaine is dying. It comes to me that she could be buried in the driveway. I do not know what the names of those trees are. It would be so easy for the family to visit her. They could back out and turn around.

"Aunt Germaine," I say, "what's the name of this place?"

Aunt Germaine does not answer.

Instead she takes her chopsticks and pinches at the dust in the light that comes into the room from everywhere seizing the pieces that are smallest.

IS THIS A LAND, A CONTINENT, CAN IT BE CONQUERED?

*A*ll of the dogs are missing. Some say the ghost of Bolivar has come back and that with that Indian Tinajaca he has done a clean sweep of this town and they have taken all of our dogs to go and conquer new worlds.

Is this where the dogs have gone? Or were taken?

I look up at snowcapped Pico Bolivar, and it looks whiter than ever, and I think that all of our white-eared dogs have gone up there to sit and do some powwowing about how they are going to do something about teaching our children not just the story of Bolivar, but the story of Bolivar, Tinajaca, and Nevado, the dog who went along with them across the Andean Paramos.

The teachers in our town keep getting drunk and driving off the side of the mountain road. What the children have learned is how to build crosses—they bring the crosses to where the teachers went off the road, and they leave lilies with the crosses.

I have been asking everyone in town where they think our dogs have gone.

This is what Mercedes thinks.

Mercedes thinks the dogs were all captured to sell by the roadside to turistas who want to take back to their countries a little of our legend.

This is what Sanchez thinks.

Sanchez thinks our dogs are still around and have never left us and points to the hills with his cane and says, "See, there are the dogs." But what Sanchez is pointing at is grazing sheep.

This is what Victoria thinks. Victoria thinks the dogs have all lost their minds and have gone down south to Barinas to sit and spy on the monkeys.

Victoria likes to tell us of how there was a time when she stayed in a hotel in Barinas that had a pool and that at nights moths as big as dogs flapped softly by her ears, whispering to her that she was special in life.

Tatuaje tills the land with the help of his oxen and talks to me while he whips them. Tatuaje and his oxen turn the dirt over, moving in spirals up toward the snowcapped peak. Them moving in spirals changes the color of the land from color to color.

"It's the cats I wish would get up and go," Tatuaje says. "They shit in my overturned land, and cat shit is not like dog shit, cat shit is shit that kills. The dogs, they are all right," says Tatuaje. "Mine got up and left too. I named him El Negro. Everyone else was calling their white-eared dogs Snowflake," Tatuaje says and goes back to whipping his oxen.

Mercedes is out on the road trying to get a ride. She wants to go into Mucuchies and see if our dogs are there being sold by men with signs that read, "Take home a piece of our history."

Even from this far away and from the back you can still see enough of the blotches Mercedes has on her legs, which is the carrying-child malady of geography because the blotches look like Asia, like Africa and like here itself.

The way Victoria talks about Barinas, I wouldn't mind going there myself. I imagine lengthy talks with moths. Maybe the moths are the ones who could tell us where the dogs have gone. Maybe the moths would whisper to us that our dogs have gone to other nations to loosen the bonds of state. Victoria says, "No, more likely than not, it's the Cock of the Rock who would be able to tell us where our dogs have gone."

"But, Victoria," I say, "no one in the past ten years in the world has seen this cock of the rock."

"I know," Victoria says, "but in Barinas I have seen one in a cloud forest where it flew above me and then came down to tell me that I was a genius of inordinate dimension."

At night, snowcapped Pico Bolivar is so white that it almost gives off light enough for me to read by.

So far none of the books in our town is missing. It is believed that if the dogs are up there powwowing, they did not need to read while they did it. But because of no dogs and no teachers, our town has begun to feel badly for the children anyway even if we have the books.

But the children are doing all right anyway. They have been seen huddling under the serape of Sanchez. At least they do not have to look at the person with the child-carrying malady of geography until she comes back.

"This is where solitude is fearsome," Tatuaje says to me as we walk along the skirt of the hills that surround Pico Bolivar. Around us are the yellow frailejones whose tapered leaves wave like fingers in the wind or like plants growing under water, floating in the tide.

"Up here we are at the bottom of the sea," Tatuaje says.

We climb the belt of the hill.

Here there are no more frailejones.

Things do not grow this high.

We walk through a mist so heavy our hair hangs like vines.

"Tell us we are special in life," Tatuaje says. "Tell us we have vision, foresight, hindsight, grasp of knowledge, play of logic, true capabilities, wealth of information, sexual prowess, supreme finesse at table."

There is no telling what the new teacher Enrique is teaching our children. It could be that his most valuable lessons are taught with Mercedes flat on her back on top of the teacher's desk. It could be that he fingers her affliction and croons to her as follows: "What is this? Is this a land? Can it be conquered? Is it known? What are its reaches?"

"Our dogs are not up here," Tatuaje says. "The howling is just the wind. If you were one of our dogs, you would not be here," Tatuaje says. "You would be down south of here perched in some tree with the monkey and cocks of the rocks, the moths whispering to you that you were once famous, once victorious, once envied for having been brave. You would be sowing your oats and resting your laurels," Tatuaje says. "You would not be up here so high where everything has ceased to grow and snow caps the mountains of the Andes."

Mercedes dreams that the dogs have all been christianized in foreign lands.

Victoria sweats and licks her arm to taste the salt.

Our dogs are missing. Tatuaje and I have gone to the top of Pico Bolivar and we did not see them. We heard howling. But Tatuaje said it was not our dogs but other dogs. Now the silence here on the paramos is complete.

LAKE MOHICAN

We are driving for rabbits. In a paper my husband has seen rabbits for free a few towns over. We get to a house that has land enough for horses and rabbits. The mother sends her children to show us the rabbits. She is at work sharpening an ax on a stone to cut the head off a chicken. My husband is off in the field, trying to ride the family's donkey. The mother rabbit is called Salt and the father rabbit is called Pepper. The children showing us the rabbit say they have not named the babies because they don't know any more names for rabbits. My husband and I decide on the rabbits we will take home. To thank the mother, we have to wait because she is killing a chicken. The chicken's head falls off. We say thank you.

The rabbits we pick die fast. One morning we wake up because the rabbits are screaming and our children are screaming.

On the floor there is blood and white fur and one of my children is picking it up, holding it as if she thought she could make the rabbit alive again by picking it up. I go after it with cleaner and a mop. But the blood stays on the floor as if it was worked into the linoleum by the manufacturer.

We eat on the slate table by a lake. My husband puts nasturtiums in the salad, and the children ask if you can die from eating flowers. My husband says he saw a man eat roses and then later the man put his hand down his throat and took out a bunny.

After dinner we go into the boat to visit the small island in the middle of the lake. I row and the children and my husband bend over the side and drag their hands in the water. There is nothing on the little island. The trees that are on it are the same kinds of trees we have all around our house. I want to burn them - and all the other trees too.

My husband swims in the lake. The children and I sit the wrong way on chairs and watch him swimming. He swims out to the middle and never looks back. He is moving along and in the light it is hard to tell if he even is a man anymore.

"He'll be late for the train," I say.

The children go out and the girls' nightgowns glow white in the morning light. I see my husband swimming for the island in the middle. Then he stands in the shallow water and he walks onto shore. I go out and stand next to my children.

"Wave," I say.

We wave.

Maybe my husband does not see us. He walks into the island's trees.

When my husband comes back from work he has a bruise on his head.

"Someone threw a rock," he says.

Tonight it is warm and the clouds are low and we are all in the garden picking nasturtiums for our salad. I am looking out at the sunset, thinking what it is that gives them streaks of color when my husband touches my arm. After dinner all of us swim out to the island and lie down on the shore. We fall asleep. We are still sleeping.

THE WOMAN IN THE
LEOPARD-SPOTTED ROBE

*M*y mother died drunk standing in the rain wearing a leopard-spotted robe. She gave way at the knees at a rising creek and fell against a Spanish moss whose ropy leaves slapped her in the face. Dead, the woman lay curled in the crap.

Afterward, when the creek was down and the sun was up, my sister and I let our mother's leopard-spotted robe dry. It still smelled of her perfume. My sister opened all the doors and all the windows just to send a breeze through the house that would get the smell of our mother out.

"It seems," my sister said, "that either every day she comes back to life or dies again."

Here, by this creek, is where my mother died. My mother died with me hardly knowing. I waved to her, thinking, "Oh, God, take this drunk woman in out of the rain."

My mother used to mew with vodka.

"What are you doing?" I once asked her when she was mewing, and she said to me, "This is so I know I am not dead."

My sister drove us up two wheels onto a stone wall one night. It had snowed so hard it did not even sound as if we had hit a stone wall. My mother had fallen onto me and her hair had gotten caught in my coat's zipper. We stood in the trees while I tried to free my mother from my coat. At times my mother's hair would stand up like soft arm hair or it would float back and forth like a sea plant moved by a current. But this time my mother's hair did not float or stand up but stayed stuck to my zipper, and the more she pulled away from me to let go of her hair, the more her hair twisted thin and the more it began to look to me like a tail and as if my mother was a rat trying to free herself to the dark of the woods.

"Libértè moi!" my mother screamed.

My sister was kicking the tires.

"A lime," my mother said.

"Lemon, Mamon," my sister said.

"Oh, all right," my mother said, "What do I know? Your sister had made me bald and now my brains are stiff with cold."

"Let's walk," I said.

"She can't walk," my sister said, meaning my mother who was pulling out the hair that was still caught in my zipper and trying to smooth it out onto the top of her head.

"I have seen the black beaches," my mother said. "I have seen the ancient ruins, the hollows in the dirt where rooms once were. Steps dug out of walls were beds and columned places were where ceremonies were once held. There is a lover's place. In this lover's place, a man and a woman lie down with each other."

My mother's head was leaned against a pipe and she was sitting on the toilet seat.

"Mamon?" I said.

But she did not answer.

I was sitting on the floor, my back leaning up against the bathroom wall. I reached out and put my hand on my mother's knee and moved her knee back and forth.

"Mamon," I said again. "Mamon, it's time to go," I said.

My mother mewed and lifted up her head. But it didn't stay up for long and fell back behind her.

Outside it was raining. The window was open. Drops splashed in and came down on us, falling on my mother's head.

"Cherie?" she said and lifted up her head.

"Oui?" I said.

"Je suis morte," she said, and touched her wet cheeks.

"Allez, Mamon. Allez," I said, and then I lifted my mother with one hand and with the other hand I pulled her pants up around her wrinkled belly.

"Yeu, c'est vous?" she said.

"No, c'est moi," I said.

My mother rocked back and forth and then her knees gave out and she landed back down on the toilet seat with her eyes closed. From the church down the street I could hear the bells ringing. It was Christmas Eve.

"Joyeux Noel," my mother said with her eyes still closed.

My mother mewed with vodka and then said, "Cherie, you were never loved."

I had made a turkey. No one was eating it. It's meat was dry and I hadn't made gravy. I poured my mother more vodka.

"Where is your husband now?" my mother said to me.

My mother straightened the green-stoned ring on her finger.

"The stone is always twisting around," she said, "but it's a good ring. I've strung strings through it and held it over mothers-to-be. Keep this ring when I'm dead," she said.

My mother told me that she had been everywhere.

"There I watched the old women in their skirts sit where the waves die down at the shore and where the children stand and splash each other," she said. "I have watched the men sit on their stools in the palm-roofed barns and calling to their skinny dogs. The waves everywhere are good for drowning," she said. "They come high and beat you down low."

My mother did not die in the water. She died sitting on the toilet.

My mother told me that she had not been anywhere.

"I have not seen the temples whose roots are overgrown with vines," she said. "I have not seen rock and stone so old that it could die. I have not seen anything."

My mother died in the middle of the night with the light on and a glass of vodka on the bathroom floor. She died and nothing else died. The icebox still made its ice and the heat pipes still heated.

In the car my mother started to pull out the rest of the hairs on her head.

"I can't take it any more, these few strands stick out like sour thumbs, better to have none than a few left to remind you of what it once was," she said.

"Sour thumbs, Mamon?" I said.

"So sour," my mother said.

My mother died looking old with no hair on top of her head and wearing her dirty leopard-spotted robe, the matching belt yanked from its loops and lost somewhere years ago.

My mother died with her eyes wide open, staring down at her green-stoned ring as if she had never seen it in her life.

ABALONE, EBONY AND TUSK

I think I can see the men with sticks turn around to look at me as they walk behind the white cows. I think I can see the men's teeth. Their teeth are whiter than the cows who have stains at the bottoms of their legs from walking through the mud.

Outside, I can see the doctor coming on board. He holds the sheets he will use to wrap up my hands. This day the sun is red. I am not sure if it is morning or evening. The doctor does not knock and he comes into my cabin without a word of hello. I am the first to talk.

"Have you see the white cows?" I ask him. I think that maybe he hasn't heard me because he does not answer and instead he puts his hand over my head. I think maybe that I have died and next he will shut my eyes for me.

"I have told you before, I see the white cows every day," the doctor says.

"And the men walking behind them with the sticks?" I say.

"They are always with the white cows," the doctor says.

"Tell me again how the legs of the cows are black with mud," I say. The doctor unwraps the sheets and I can feel the air beginning to touch my hands.

"You've been at your hands," he says.

"No, I haven't."

"You must be doing it in your sleep," he says.

"I dream," I say.

"You must dream that your hands are rid of this rash. Dream of abalone, ebony, or tusk, those are smooth," he says and he takes out a tin and with two fingers he pulls up the yellow fat and spreads it onto my hands.

"I've slid down the elephant's trunk," I say. "I've held its ears for balance when stepping to the ground."

"Next time we'll use lemon juice," the doctor says, "to draw the pus and dry the rash."

"Tell me," I say to the doctor, "how the men bend down and with leaves they wet in the river, they wash down the muddied legs of the white cows."

The doctor takes the old sheets from my hands and he throws them out the window into the ocean but I cannot hear them hit the water. He puts his tin of fat back into his robes and he says, "I will come back late at night and I will bring you to the shores of India and you will see the white cows and I will sit you on an elephant so that you can slide down its long gray trunk, but for now you must dream that your hands, like the hooves of the white cows are strong and can take you anywhere."

After the doctor leaves I sleep and dream I am a white cow. I see the streets of India as I turn from side to side. At my back a stick pushes me so I do not stop for long to watch the things I see on the streets of India.

Under his robes I touch the Indian doctor's belly. I want to see if Indian skin feels like my skin.

"Are the sheets slipping off your hands?" he asks me.

"No," I say. I have forgotten about my hands being in sheets because we are now in the small boat and the doctor is rowing and my head is on the middle of his chest and every time his arms go back and then forward to row the boat it feels as if he is just about to put his arms all the way around me and to hold me, but he doesn't and his arms go back again to pull the oars through the air so he can once again pull them through the ocean and we are on our way to India.

"There are the white cows," the doctor says to me and I cannot look because I think he is not telling me the truth and like his arms almost coming around me in the row boat but never coming full around, I will never see the white cows with the men walking behind them, pushing the white cows with the sticks on down the road.

"Look," the doctor says and he takes me out from under his robes and I stand barefoot and I think how good the dust and the small rocks on the ground feel on my feet.

I look ahead and I see the white cows. But in the moonlight the cows do not look white and instead they look silver and I say to the doctor, "These cows are not from India." And the doctor asks me what do I mean and I tell him that cows I have heard of are white and are not silver looking like they have been sent down from the moon. The doctor tells me that I have been looking out from my bed on the ship at the moon too many nights now to know white from silver.

"How can this be India?" I think. My hands itch and wrapped in sheets I rub them together. It may be that the animal fat has been rubbed on so many times that my hands are becoming paws, or better yet hooves.

"What are you doing to me?" I ask the doctor.

He takes me up under his robes and then he unties his pants and we go down to lie on the ground. I can see out through the neck of his robes - I can see the men with the sticks pushing the white cows on down the road.

India, Indian my doctor. Shaman, tassel-booted dancing medicine man. Seer seeing me girl gone woman going old. Sheet wrapper. Animal fat spreader. Robe wearer. Turban-headed healer.

My doctor cures. I am sick. From this boat he has brought me back to my hands rash. "Rotter," I am. I yell out holed windows. What about the elephants? The cows? The rides, the ears and the tails? I look at my hands. They are green. Mother pulls back the blanket and finds a pebble.

"Did this come out of you?" she asks. "I'll call the doctor," she says.

"The doctor," I say. Tarot deck carrying, Prince of Darkness learned, future schooled and top casinoed.

Mother tweezers out the pebble and puts it on a plate. Rolling it rolls like a number's game ball filling a betted place, winning for black suited chip turning men.

"I can't get land," Mother says. Back goes the ship-to-shore to cradle.

"My little girl," she says. "You've got a fever."

"You have a gun, Mother." She holds my foot.

"Sleep," she says. She twirls the gun on her finger. Vested she sizes me up, down from the head to my toes she goes eyeing. I could be a drawer of considerable speed. Watch out, Mother. I too am holstered, swung out from saloon doors countless times, nights tequila heavy from men's pores sweating over bordello bed springs, whored, de-watered, brawl-minded, fist-readied, duke-abled men. Mother, I can fight.

"Angel," she says.

"Look, there are more pebbles," I say. I take her hand to go pebbling on the surface of my bed.

"You are hot," Mother says.

The waves are dogs wanting to come in. There are breeds of waves we do not know. Unpedigreed they jump our shipsides, lap our hull.

"Get a stick, Mother," I say.

"I am trying the doctor," Mother says.

"Is this the doctor," Mother says.

I hold the pebble. The pebble is veined.

Soothsayer, snake tail rattler, dried leaf shaker, swami, charmer, mortar-pestle-India-Indian Man where are the cows? Where are the elephants now?

"Holding for the doctor," Mother says.

I have your eyes, Mother. I have your legs, Mother. I have your hands, Mother. I have your tongue, Mother.

"How soon?" Mother says. "When?" Mother says.

"I can't wait," Mother says.

Mother, have you climbed down the elephant's trunk? Held its ears for balance when stepping to the ground?

"Doctor?" Mother says.

Mother, your legs are mine. We have gone to the same places. Waded in the river. Touched cows' white haunches. Mother, if you are speaking, I am speaking. Mother, if you are walking, I am walking. Mother, we can go anywhere. Indiaward we are headed.

Mother opens up the window and looks out. The windows here are round.

Mother, I am like you. Your dark eyes and hair, your never knowing where you just came from on a street or a road. Your cooking talents, your shaking leg, your widow's peak, your cowlick, your cheekbones, your mole, your square shoulders.

"Here comes the doctor," Mother says. Mother shuts the round window glass. Her hair is all over the place and it looks like she has been on the deck of this boat in a storm rather than down here in a cabin with a girl whose hands have been rubbed with fat, wrapped in sheets, and then tied.

A dog has jumped on board. Wet, he has slid down the halls and is at our door, shaking out the salt water, his tail slapping the wood, his paws against the doorframe, his mouth and teeth around the knob - I can see it turning from my bed.

"Come in," Mother says, and opens the cabin door.

LEGACIES

*R*ad is my eldest. Then comes Betty, Nicole and Alexis. They all want to know what it is I will die with. Their way of finding out is taking everything that I have and seeing what it is I will say no to them for taking. Rad takes tables, dressers and chairs. Betty took the cameo. Nicole took the pearls. Alexis got Mary without the chain. They keep asking me what if the house catches on fire—what will it be for that I run back into the burning house for?

What I've got in my house that I like are chips in the paint. Coats upon coats without scraping worked in have prepared my walls for grand-scale chipping. I think every time I come home or leave the house and shut the door that pictures get their chance to break through. My walls are expressive. Figures graze and trees dot. Silos stand alone. Sometimes they come out friendly next to farmhouses. I've got crops and flying birds. Before I turn out the light, I look to see what is new on my walls. Birds show fast, a new one almost every week. I think a mountain is coming. I'm waiting for a farmer man. His head broke through today. Come weeks, come months, if his legs and arms don't come too, I'll cheat and peel away to make him known.

I go to have my toes straightened out. What is found from the picture of my foot is foreign matter floating in tissue. I tap at my foot. I try to ruck up foreign matter - get it passaged to other places within me, coax it, speak to it in a language it knows, move it out the region of nerves that has made me think all these years I have been suffering from China.

They have found no point of entry.

"Not to worry," I am told, "it's negligible."

Metal ridden, I steer for the refrigerator put it on where the foreign matter is rooted inside me, seeing if like the easy way it must have slid through me I can draw it out. But this metal is stuck deep. I stare at the bridge through my window. I hear the cars driving. I listen to the steel mesh.

Farmer man at home is changing shape. No longer does the peel look as if a man will show through but a woman maybe, maybe a milkmaid on her way to do chores. Maybe a bandannaed potato-eater from something Van Gogh. Girth is what's showing through first. Aproned hips and wood shoes. She is as tall as the wall's tallest tree. She stands like the owner of these fields, these streams, these walls, this house.

The metal is taken from my foot. The surgeon gives it to me to take home. When my children come over, they ask for it.

"Take it," I say. "Who needs a chalice?" I say and I look at my walls.

WHITELY ON THE TIPS

Wade Byrd had light like never before. The oak that once stood in his neighbor's yard was gone. After its roots had spread and weakened the walls of their home, the neighbors cut the oak down. Now the California sun came into Wade Byrd's living room where only days ago green leaves and branches had blocked the harsh light.

Wade Byrd could see for the first time in his living room motes of dust floating in the air and for the first time he could feel the warm sun on his face. He could even feel the light warming his chest through his plaid shirt and tee-shirt. When Wade Byrd became too hot he took off his plaid shirt and sat in his tee-shirt which was yellow with age and almost see-through. When he looked down at himself he could see a swirl of his gray chest hairs matted beneath the cotton cloth.

Wade Byrd wished for the oak to somehow come back. It now lay in so many sized logs on his neighbors' lawn waiting to be hauled away. He imagined, for a moment, going out in the night and re-stacking the logs, erecting the great big oak so that once again it could provide shade.

Wade Byrd never took much notice of the neighbors before they cut the oak down, but now that the tree was in pieces on their front lawn, he could see when the neighbors came home and when they left. He could see the woman come out of her house with file folders held to her chest in the mornings before she unlocked her car door and drove away. In the evenings he could see the man walking from the mailbox looking through the mail in his hand, not watching his step as he went.

The man sold candy and once he offered some to Wade Byrd. The candy was suckers that came in sour flavors. The sucker Wade Byrd took tasted like black pepper and Wade Byrd held it up to the light, looking for black flecks, but he did not see any.

The neighbors had a dog and when the neighbors came home they would let the dog out and it would sleep on the front doorstep. It seemed a good dog to Wade Byrd. It never barked unless a stranger came up the walk or pulled into the driveway. Even then it was only just one or two barks and then the dog would lie back down again. The dog still lay on the front doorstep, but now that the oak was cut down the dog panted. The dog's tongue hung out, touching the cement doorstep and the dog never seemed to be asleep and sometimes Wade Byrd thought he could hear the dog sigh.

Wade Byrd decided to plant new grass on his lawn. It was timothy grass, the same grass his family had once grown in front of their house in New Hampshire where he had lived as a boy. Wade Byrd thought that maybe having the same kind of grass would remind him of the way frost sat whitely on the tips of the tall grass on cold fall mornings.

The dog slept on its front doorstep while Wade Byrd took the timothy grass seeds and shook them loose so that they fell between his held open fingers. A neighbor girl came down the street. The girl skipped up to the dog on the front doorstep. She crouched down beside the dog. She held onto it by the neck, hugging it and then pulling the dog's neck back so she could do something. Maybe kiss the dog, Wade Byrd thought.

The dog growled. Wade Byrd saw the dog turns its head. He saw the dog bite the girl. At first the girl held her hands up to her face, and then she screamed. Wade Byrd ran over to the girl and with timothy grass seeds still in one hand he tried to move the girl's hands away from her face.

"Let's have a look," he said to the girl. The timothy grass seeds that were on his hands stuck to her wrists that were covered in blood.

Under the girl's eye was a gash and on her forehead was a puncture wound. He led the girl to one of the oak logs on the lawn. He had the girl sit on the upright log. He could smell the fresh smell of the sawed open oak. He could see the fine sawdust lay as if sprinkled over the rings of the tree.

He took off his plaid shirt and leaned over her in his yellow tee-shirt. With his plaid shirt he wiped the blood that was pouring from the wounds on her face.

"You'll need a stitch or two," he said. The girl nodded. Her hair fell into her face and a strand of it became slick with blood. Wade Byrd looked around. Where are the man and the woman? he thought. They must have heard the girl's screams. The dog was still on the front doorstep. Wade Byrd could see that he was no longer panting. He was finally asleep.

"Sit tight," Wade Byrd said. He went into his house and came outside with his cordless phone. He had never gone so far with the phone before. He had only ever gone from room to room in his house with it. He wondered if it would work on the neighbors' front lawn. He stood in front of the girl. She was rocking herself back and forth on the oak log.

"Better call your mother," Wade Byrd said.

The girl dialed. There was no one home.

"It's the answering machine," the girl said.

"Leave a message. Tell her you're okay. Tell her you're being taken to the hospital here in town and that she can find you in the emergency room."

After the girl left the message, she handed the phone back to Wade Byrd. When he took it he saw that the girl had left small fingerprints of blood on the phone.

Wade Byrd turned around and looked at the neighbors' house. For a moment Wade Byrd could see the woman standing behind the curtain. When she saw Wade Byrd, she quickly moved away.

"Hey!" Wade Byrd said. He waved at the plate glass picture window in the man and woman's living room, but no one reappeared from behind the curtain.

Making sure the girl kept his plaid shirt pressed to her wounds, Wade Byrd then left the girl and walked up to the man and woman's front door. The dog did not wake up. Wade Byrd thought that the last time he had seen the dog sleeping so soundly was before the oak had been cut down and there had been shade on the front doorstep. Wade Byrd stepped over the dog and rang the door's buzzer. After a while, he started knocking on the door. Blood on his knuckles left small stains on the wood.

"Hello! Hello!" he said. He jiggled the door handle, but it was locked.

Wade Byrd turned around and went back to the girl.

"Let's go," he said to the girl and helped her into his car.

He wanted to lay her down on the back seat, but first he had to clear away some bags of timothy seed and plant fertilizer, and he had to wipe the dust off the seat with his hand. He could not remember the last time someone else rode with him in his car. When she lay down he placed a bag of timothy seed under her head for a pillow.

It was a short ride to the hospital in town. Wade Byrd drove slowly and kept turning around to look at the girl as he drove. Wade Byrd drove with the windows down because it was such a hot day. He was thankful, in a way, that the girl had needed his plaid shirt to soak up her blood because he knew that it would have been too hot to be wearing both the plaid shirt and his tee shirt.

Wade Byrd liked having company in his car. He had forgotten what that was like. He wondered, for a second, how far he could ride with the girl in his back seat. For a moment he thought that driving the girl around in his car was like his cordless phone, there was only so far he could go with the girl lying down on his back seat before it did not work.

"I shouldn't have hugged that dog," the girl said when they were stopped at a light.

"No, I guess you shouldn't have," Wade Byrd said.

"But he looked sad," the girl said.

Wade Byrd nodded. He had in fact thought the same thing about the dog earlier in the day, when he had seen the dog trying to sleep on the front doorstep.

"It was the heat. He couldn't sleep," Wade Byrd said to the girl.

Winters in New Hampshire Wade Byrd, like the other boys his age, would just wear a thermal shirt and a vest when they would go ice-skating or walk in the woods. He was never cold. In the summer, he was never hot. He and his friends would go to each others' houses and eat dinner on a breezy screened in porch. He and his mother and father knew everyone in town. They knew everyone's dog in town too and if a girl were to get bit in his town, why, Wade Byrd thought, the whole town would have come out to help the girl, especially the people who owned the dog.

Wade Byrd took the girl to the emergency wing. When he saw the mother come running into the hospital towards the girl and screaming, Wade Byrd left. He went back to his car that looked white with glare from the sun as it sat in the hot asphalt covered parking lot.

In order to drive home, he would have to drive in the direction where the sun was setting. It would hurt his eyes just to see the road. He decided to drive in the other direction instead. He did not know where he was going. He drove onto the freeway, away from the sun.

He drove for a few hours until he had to stop for gas. He looked around, trying to see where he was. He had not paid attention to signs along the way. It was night and he was somewhere out in the desert. The air was cool. He could see some stars. He did not get back on the freeway. He drove his car to the side of road and stopped. He rolled the windows down, letting the desert wind come through. It sent up into the air some loose seeds of timothy grass that were on the seat. Would they take root here in the dry desert ground? He imagined a field of timothy grass beside him where now there was just rocks and dirt.

Wade Byrd noticed he was cold. Finally, he was cold. He put his head back and fell asleep. When he awoke it was still cold, but the night was coming to an end. The sun would soon come up in the east. Wade Byrd did not want to continue in that direction. He did not want his eyes to hurt in the sun. He drove the other way. He drove west toward his home where he had left his cordless telephone out on the oak log of the neighbor's lawn and where he would have to watch the woman every morning with the file folders pressed to her chest make her way to her car and watch the man who sold sour candy suckers walk back from his mailbox, looking through his letters. He would have to watch the dog catchers from the city come and place a metal loop on a long pole around the dog's neck to get him into their truck so they could drive the dog to wherever it was they would kill him. Wade Byrd would watch the gardeners of the man and woman come with a pick-up truck and haul the oak logs away. All that would be left of the oak would be splinters, woven into the grass blades of their lawn. He would watch his timothy grass grow and then burn in the hot sun that remained hot all summer and into November. Wade Byrd would become angry now too. He thought maybe his anger would come from the heat, and that like the dog, he would do something that no one expected him to do. Maybe someday he would come at a full run and crash through the man and the woman's plate glass window, the window with the curtains the woman hid behind when the girl was bit by their dog. The glass would then smash into pieces, coming down like a shower of ice all around him.

REAL ENOUGH

❧

*J*im Crowley wore his bearskin rug. The head of the bear sat on top of the head of Jim Crowley. Jim Crowley looked in the hall mirror. He fixed the bearskin rug so that it covered more of his shoulders and so that the eyes on the bear looked straight ahead.

Outside, by the lake, Jim Crowley patted the sides of the bearskin rug and thought if there were light to see by he could watch the dust rise up from the old fur and get carried out over the lake in the night breeze.

Across the lake there was a summer camp with an Indian name. He used to find arrowheads there on that side of the lake when he was a boy. All he would have to do was walk barefoot through the grass a ways and he would feel one sharp beneath him.

Jim Crowley got into his rowboat. The nails on the paws of the bearskin clattered on the aluminum sides of the boat as he lowered himself onto the bench seat.

Jim Crowley rowed to the middle of the lake, every once in a while stopping to keep the bearskin rug from slipping off his shoulders.

If he were not rowing, Jim Crowley thought the boat on the water would not move. There was no breeze and the lake seemed like a thing that never moved and that it was not the same lake by Jim Crowley's house that lapped the shore and splashed against the old dock's legs.

Jim Crowley rowed the boat to the other side. The Indian summer camp side. He brought the boat up partway onto shore and then he walked toward where the cabins were and where the children were sleeping inside them.

Jim Crowley opened the screen door of one cabin. He started searching. He opened cubbies and went through shorts' pockets, pulling out candy wrappers, toy cars and then he went to them in their sleep and started prying open their small hands.

There was one boy who slept by the window and a light from outside shone on him. The boy's hand was closed and Jim Crowley opened it and inside he found what he had come looking for and he took it. Jim Crowley took off the bearskin and covered the boy with it. The head of the bear covered the head of the boy. Then Jim Crowley left the cabin.

Jim Crowley tried to remember how the bear had run before he had shot it. He could not remember if the bear had looked around. He could remember it both ways, he could remember seeing the bear turning around and looking at him and he could remember the bear running straight for him. He was not sure which way to remember was right. He remembered his father saying he had better do the cutting and his father cut the bear open and gave him the liver to hold. Jim Crowley remembered standing in the field and holding the warm liver and looking at the sun. The father took his knife and cut and tore the fat from the bear's skin.

"He'll have glass for eyes, you'll see, Jim, he'll look real enough to shoot again when we're done with him," his father had said.

Jim Crowley told his father that the liver was hard to hold.

It felt like it was some kind of animal trying to get away and run off back into the woods.

At the shore Jim Crowley climbed quietly into his row boat and started back towards his side of the lake. While rowing, he sang "Johnny Appleseed." At his dock he tied up his boat, singing "For giving me the things I need, the sun and the rain and the apple seed."

Inside his house he walked upstairs to his bedroom. What Jim Crowley first noticed in his bedroom was the moonlight shining on a clean place on the floor where the bear skin had once been. The clean space showed the outline of the bear looking straight at him and he wondered if he had placed the rug there that way because maybe that was the right way, the way he remembered the bear running straight at him when he first shot it. He sat down in the middle of the clean space and opened his hand, looking at the arrowhead he had taken from the boy. The point was sharp and could have, Jim Crowley thought, been knife enough for him to have cut open the bear and torn the fat from the bear's skin if his father hadn't already taken the task upon himself.

In the morning, grace began in the dining hall. Counselors and campers bowed their heads and the boy looked to see if he could see his new face, the face of the bear, in a plate scratched dull by other campers' forks from years before.

OUR UNDERWATER MOTHER

"*T*ell us a love story," the children said, and the mother took a drink of her drink and started to tell. "Wait," the children said to their mother. "That's not how it goes," they said. "Tell us when the woman took off her head and started brushing her hair. Tell us about the spirit who clawed through the thatched roof. Tell us when the car filled up with roses you couldn't see in the windows. Tell us things like that," the children said.

The mother took another drink of her drink and wiped her mouth with the back of her hand.

"I only know one story," the mother said.

"No, you don't at all," the children said. "You know more. Tell us what happened to you."

The children went under water to look at the scars on their mother's knees and they touched the scars and they said to their mother, "Tell us about these."

Outside a fire burned.

"Go ahead," the children said, "tell us," and they hit the sides of the trunk they were bathing in.

The mother saw her children in the orange light from the fire. When her children spoke, they showed black spaces in their mouths made from newly missing teeth.

"I give up," the mother said. "What is it that I know?"

"The rabbits," the children said. "The birds, the chickens, the dogs."

"Greece," the mother said, "I have never even gone."

"No," the children said, "Greece was the lava, the man, and the woman."

"All that I saw of India was its shores," the mother said.

"What about the cows?" the children said.

"This I got on a fence," the mother said, showing them a scar. "This from a fall," showing them another.

"No," said the children. "We already know about those. Those are China. Those are from the men with swords."

"That hurts," the mother said, and she pushed the hands of her children away from her knees.

The fire burned trash. Soot floated up and into the windows.

The children put their arms around their mother's neck. "What about this?" they said and they touched the mark she had near her ear.

"I don't know. I can't see it," the mother said.

"Tell us about it," the children said.

The mother asked for her drink and the children held it to her mouth.

"Tell us about Spain," they said. "Tell us about the man who held his own hand."

"I only know this," the mother said, and she started to tell her story.

Outside sirens for other fires wailed close by but then trailed off down the streets. The fire that lit up their place in orange light sounded like people fed it with cans that, when the cans hit what it was that the fire was burning, made a cowbell sound.

"This is not about love," the children said to their mother and they fitted their heads under the water, rinsing out soap that came to the top in bubbles and floated over the metal latches of the trunk and into keyholes.

"I miss those days," the mother said.

With the mother in the trunk, the water rose.

"Be careful," said the children. "It would be terrible if there were no more water!"

Perched on the sides of the trunk the children lifted up the washcloth and squeezed its water out onto their mother's back. When the children neared the mark, they said, "We are going to wash it away."

"And these," the children said, "we'll get them too," and they took turns going under the water, looking for the scars with the washcloth in their hands. The mother drank her drink and watched her children's hair float up onto the top of the water.

"Nights on Lake Mohican we fished for eels," the mother said.

"What about the chickens?" the children said. "The doves. The man who ate the flowers?"

"Some nights," the mother said, "eels were scarce and pickerel was the only thing we caught."

"What about the thorns?" the children said. "What about the love story?" they said. "What about the garden with the corn?"

"Take care," the mother said.

The children pulled at the lid of the trunk.

Outside, the flames from the fire burnt out.

In darkness, the children said, "Mommy, guess what we are doing!"

"Swimming," the mother said.

"But where to?"

"To shore," the mother said.

"To Lake Mohican!" the children screamed.

In the darkness the mother could hear the latches and the hinges of the wood as the children swam around in the trunk.

"Where are we now?" the mother asked, taking a drink but missing in the darkness.

"We are floating on the lava," the children said.

"Me too," the mother said.

The children thought, "Such a thing - could it be our mother?"
And they looked around the dark kitchen.

Our underwater mother is so quiet.

We did not know our mother was so heavy. We did not know how much she wanted to stay down.

But the mother finally came up and said, "Where is my Tom Collins?" searching for her sunken glass.

One child, maybe two, the younger ones, put their heads under the water. "Can we still hear it?" they thought. "Are the words still being said?"

Her children were swollen. Their mouths open.

Outside the trash fire must have started up in the wind because the children were orange in the light. The mother thought of how there had once been a rash on her hands. There was once a view of a town from a winding road. Once there was corn in the garden.

The children shook their mother. The mother was falling asleep.

"What are you dreaming?" the children asked.

"I am being careful," the mother wanted to say, but said nothing, for now she was asleep, swimming in a lake, sleeping where a naked man swims.

DELAWARE

I carried him around for a day. I think it was almost a whole day that I carried him around with me on my shoe. It was his last wish. I took the ashes to the only cliff I knew about and threw them off. Later I looked down and I saw that there was some white shit on my shoe. It was some of the ashes, I suppose, blown back by the air, I suppose.

Unless it had just fallen there.

I'm not sure. No way I could be sure. No way anyone could be.

I can't help thinking if what was on my shoe was from here or from there - I mean from his arms or from his legs and so on. Then the other thing I can't help thinking is that almost all the places that I went to that day were places he would have probably wanted me to go to. But I don't know, maybe they weren't. Maybe I should have wiped the shit off my shoe or maybe I should have just gotten it in my pocket somehow and then gone back to the cliff and tried to throw it off again.

There is a river I've been to which has a bank that touches a graveyard for horses. If you look down into the water there, you can see spotted bones. I used to swim there. Not a lot, just enough to start feeling that swimming in deep water was a lonely thing. But, really, I didn't swim there. Not exactly. What I did there was tread water and sing at the top of my lungs. I think I wanted something to happen. I don't know what.

When I tread water, I saw part of me working so hard to keep the other part of me afloat. It made me scared. I looked down in the water at the bones. I wanted to make believe I was a crocodile in warm water who did not know the thing above me was the sun. But all I could make believe about was the bones.

I don't swim there anymore. I start thinking that my father's ashes that I threw off the cliff fell down to a stream and got to the river. He will hear me swimming again, and he will want to do something horrible to me or worse to me. He will want to say something he said to me summers before.

I am a dreamer in the water. I cannot even swim in the water. I just keep myself afloat in the water.

Sometimes I think that my father was just the word that I remember that he said.

Swimming in deep water is quiet. When I swam in the river, after I brushed the shit off my shoe, it was quiet. It was so quiet that I could have heard a cotton shift being pulled over my mother's head. I thought: This would be him.

I am waiting for little things to happen that will remind me of him. I am waiting for him to tell me to stop waiting. I am waiting for my father all over again.

READY IN THE NIGHT

❧

W ild mushrooms grow on the hotel lawn. He has seen them growing during the night as he held the curtain aside. His son has told him that you cannot see mushrooms growing, but the father has seen the white tops coming up brighter and rounder every hour, a field of rising moons.

"Sweet fucking Georgia," the son said, and stood up from where he lay on the bed and went to the toilet, leaving the door open so that his father could see how his boy undid his belt as the boy stood over the bowl and held himself in his hands.

To the father it looked as though there would be plenty of wild mushrooms, even beyond the hotel lawn clear to across the road where there were so many white birches that it looked as though snow had fallen in a forest.

In the toilet the son stepped out of his pants. His belt buckle clanked against the tub.

"I can't sleep," the son said.

When he was a boy, the father had owned white rabbits that he had had to kill. He had had to cut a hole in a shoebox and then he had started the car. The tailpipe he had fed through a hole in the shoebox. The feet of the rabbits had pressed down warmly on his hands as the rabbits turned in circles, making the shoebox tilt from side to side. Before the rabbits had died, he had lifted the lid of the box. He had never seen the rabbits moving so quickly or breathing so deeply, pushing at the air with their noses so hard that he thought that the rabbits were never going to die, that they would force their way up out of the shoebox and live forever, multiplying to untold extremes, the world tilting in the places that they walked upon.

"Where in Georgia are we?" the father said. "Are we in the heart of it?"

The father could not remember if that had been the last time that he had had to kill.

The father could lay the bedspread down, pick the wild mushrooms, and throw them onto the bedspread - then knot the corners together and carry it up to his son.

The father had had to kill a dog once. After the rabbits, he had had to kill a dog. But the father could not remember how it was that he had had to kill a dog.

"It's just Georgia," the son said.

The father wiped his face with his hand, letting the curtain fall back to cover the window again.

"Niggers and belles," the son said, and turned to hold his arms out for the woman who was not in the room.

"I am going out now," the father said.

The author wishes to acknowledge her gratitude to Dan Wickett, Steven Gillis, Steven Seighman and Judy Heiblum.

And, as always, many thanks to Gordon Lish.